They called it "THE INCIDENT"

By

J.M. JOHNSON

Copyright © 2016 J.M. Johnson

All rights reserved. No part of this publication may be reproduced, stored in or introduced into a retrieval system, or transmitted in any form, or by any means (electronic, mechanical, photocopying, recording, or otherwise) without the prior written permission of J.M. Johnson.

This book is a work of fiction. Names, (other than place names) characters, businesses, organizations and events are the product of the author's imagination or are used fictitiously. Any resemblance to actual events or persons living or dead is coincidental.

ACKNOWLEDGEMENTS

A special thank you to my friend Leda Wagner for her willingness to be the 'test' reader and for her reviewing and editing of "The Incident".

Leda wrote:

Great. I could not stop reading. The beginning was interesting enough to make me want to continue but it really picked up speed as I went along. I really did like it. And the ending as well.

Well done you talented woman you. Leda

Contents

CHAPTER ONE	3
CHAPTER TWO	9
CHAPTER THREE	19
CHAPTER FOUR	24
CHAPTER FIVE	32
CHAPTER SIX	38
CHAPTER SEVEN	45
CHAPTER EIGHT	53
CHAPTER NINE	56
CHAPTER TEN	66
CHAPTER ELEVEN	73
CHAPTER TWELVE	80
CHAPTER THIRTEEN	85
CHAPTER FOURTEEN	89
CHAPTER FIFTEEN	101
CHAPTER SIXTEEN	110
CHAPTER SEVENTEEN	115
CHAPTER EIGHTEEN	119
CHAPTER NINETEEN	129
CHAPTER TWENTY	134
CHAPTER TWENTY-ONE	143
CHAPTER TWENTY-TWO	147
CHAPTER TWENTY-THREE	152
CHAPTER TWENTY-FOUR	158
CHAPTER TWENTY-FIVE	162
CHAPTER TWENTY-SIX	167

CHAPTER TWENTY-SEVEN	171
EPILOGUE	176
About J.M Johnson	178
WHAT HAPPENED TO TARA	179

CHAPTER ONE

"Did you hear that?"

Tony looked up from his book and stilled the rocking of his chair. In the late summer twilight, the birds still sang and the breeze still whispered in the trees. But he felt a difference in the atmosphere.

He glanced toward Irma, watching her fingers flash as she wielded the crochet hook.

She looked up. "What is it?" she inquired. "Is something wrong?" She glanced around the yard then back to him.

"I don't know." He rubbed a hand through his gray hair and shook his head. "Suddenly something doesn't seem right."

They both stood and walked to the edge of the porch. Tony rested his calloused hands on the railing, noticing that it needed painting again. The same familiar flowers nudged against the side of the house. The birds tweeted their good night songs.

The old sheepdog who had been snoring loudly, reluctantly struggled to his feet and tottered after them. Tony reached down and affectionately rubbed his grey muzzle. "Stay there, Rufus," he commanded. "No need for you to get up". The dog sighed but stayed with his master.

Tony glanced towards the driveway. He could just make out the gate, almost hidden in the forest of old growth pines and firs that nudged up to the road. If he turned his head, he would see the garden with its neat rows of potatoes, cabbage and corn, just about ready for harvesting.

"Oh my goodness!" Irma gasped. "Look!" In the distant sky they could see something falling, followed by a trail of white smoke. "It's a plane!"

There was a muffled boom and they knew the plane had hit the ground. Involuntarily they grasped each other's hand.

"What should we do?" Irma looked up at him.

"We can't do anything." He turned back to the chairs. "It's too far away for us to do anything." He sat heavily. "Those poor people."

"I heard something else too, before the crash." He looked around, suddenly noticing how very quiet it had become.

"I think the power's out." Irma pulled open the screen door and clicked the porch light switch a few times.

"That's what it is," Relief washed over their faces. "The power is out, that's all."

Tony turned toward the house. "I'll bet that what I heard is the sound stopping." His voice was troubled. "We don't really hear the fridge, or the hum of appliances until they quit."

"I hope it doesn't last long." Irma's voice quavered. "It'll be full dark soon. Maybe we should find the candles."

He nodded in agreement. "I'll just check on things" he told her. "Maybe we can call some of the neighbors and see if they've heard anything." She heard him pick up the phone, then lay it back down again.

"Phone's dead too," he called through the open door. "I'll try my cell."

Irma picked up her needlework, but was too unsettled to continue. Sighing, she laid it in the basket at her feet. Without lights there was no point in going in and the evening was still warm enough that they didn't need the sweaters that were draped casually on the backs of their chairs. She leaned back and closed her eyes, letting the gentle rocking soothe her.

Tony came back shaking his head. "I don't understand it," he muttered. "phone's dead and my cell won't come on. Very strange." He cocked his head for a moment. "And listen, Mother, there is no traffic. I don't know when I've heard it be so quiet."

Only the sound of the birds broke the evening hush. The traffic on their country road was usually sparse, but now it seemed to have stopped altogether.

For the next hour, they rocked and watched the sun setting in the west. There was no need to talk. After nearly fifty years, they each knew what the other was thinking. Finally, Tony broke the silence. "I wonder if anybody was saved from the plane."

Irma nodded. "What a terrible thing. I've never seen anything like that before."

She stood up resolutely. "At least we can have tea. Thank goodness we have a propane stove to cook on."

In the kitchen, she reached for the tap, then chuckled ruefully. "Oh-oh. No electricity, no water pump."

"The power must be off everywhere," Tony commented. "if the community pump isn't working."

She lifted the kettle and felt its weight. There was enough water for tea. "do we have some matches?" she asked her husband. It was dark now and she could barely see him sitting at the table. "I'll need to light the stove manually."

She heard him rummaging in the "junk" drawer. There were usually matches in there. And candles too, she remembered.

"Here they are." Tony swung towards her, matches in hand, and collided with her shoulder. "Watch out," he cried. "It's so dark I can't see you."

"Ouch!" She rubbed her shoulder where his fist had made contact. "Can you light a candle? At least we don't have to run into each other."

Half an hour later they were drinking hot cups of tea and eating ice cream by candlelight.

"More ice cream? Irma offered. "It'll all melt by morning."

Tony shook his head and pushed the empty bowl to one side. "No, it's late. We won't solve anything sitting here worrying. Let's go to bed and in the morning everything will be back to normal."

"I don't know why I'm so nervous." She shivered slightly. "We've been without power before but this feels different somehow."

Even in the country, it was seldom completely dark in the house. Appliances hummed, clocks glowed, computer terminals shone through the night. Now everything was black and silent. Even Rufus seemed restless and kept getting up to pace the kitchen.

Tony sipped the last of his tea and stood up. "Come on, Mother." He held out his hand. "Leave the clean-up for morning. Let's go to bed. We can sleep in the dark, I'm sure. Lay down, Rufus. Nothing is going to get us tonight."

A hundred miles away, Jason and Monica Baldini were snuggled on the couch watching their favourite movie. Both were exhausted after the struggle to put their year old son to bed.

"He's getting big enough to manipulate us." Jason groaned. "He does it on purpose I'm sure."

"Don't be silly." Monica gave him a gentle punch on the shoulder. "he's just a baby and that's what babies do. They fuss and fret and need more hugs." She stretched her long legs out in front of her and yawned. "I don't think I'm going to last through this movie though. I'm going to bed."

She stood up just as the television screen went black. At the same time, they were startled by an explosion that rattled the window.

Jason leaped up and threw back the drapes. They both gasped as they saw and heard two more explosions from the nearby airport. Monica put her hands over her mouth in horror and pointed to the street, ten floors below. Cars and trucks had come to a complete halt with many of them colliding. People spilled onto the street from the vehicles and from nearby buildings.

"Quick," Jason ran for the door. "Call 911. And don't go anywhere until I come back."

"Where are you going?" Frantically Monica grabbed for her cell phone and began to stab at the numbers. "There won't be an elevator."

The door had slammed behind him, as Monica realized there was no dial tone. She frowned and put it down on the counter, then reached for the house phone. It too was silent.

Below her, she saw Jason run out of the building and make his way to the nearest car. He spoke briefly to the woman standing beside the driver's door then moved on to the next one. Up and down the street, others were doing the same. Outside one small car that appeared to have collided with a pickup, she could see a woman lying on the ground. Several people huddled around her. Smoke drifted lazily in the distance.

Monica stood, mesmerized by the scene below. Tears ran down her face, unnoticed. She lost sight of her husband and watched as people slowly drifted away from the street. Some men had picked up the woman and carried her into a nearby building. She wondered if the person was alive. Why wasn't help coming? No sirens wailed; no emergency lights flashed. Finally, she glanced around the dark apartment. How long had she been standing there? Reflexively she glanced at the clock on the microwave. Shaking her head, she looked at the watch ticking on her wrist. "Midnight!" Suddenly afraid, she checked the locks on the outer door. There was a security chain that had never been used since they moved in two years ago. Now she slid the chain into its slot and rotated the handle on the deadbolt. Without street lights or the usual traffic, the apartment was as black as a cave. She pulled the sofa over to the window, determining to keep watch until Jason returned. Feeling cold, she pulled the blanket that was draped over the arm of the couch, over her shoulders. Outside, it was now too dark to see what was happening on the street.

Wearily, she rested her head on a cushion and prayed that everybody was home safe.

CHAPTER TWO

After a restless night, Irma shuffled around the kitchen in her slippers, wondering if she had enough water for the morning coffee. It was early, the sun was barely above the horizon. She glanced at her wristwatch.

Four a.m. That seemed right but without confirmation, she felt disoriented. Usually, the radio would be on, telling her the time, the weather and how the traffic was flowing in the city.

"It's amazing," she thought to herself as she filled the coffee pot from bottles of water, "how dependant we are on someone telling us the sun is shining and it will be a nice day."

She stopped pouring the water realizing there would be no coffee made in this pot until the power came back on.

Just then, Tony came into the kitchen. He laughed when he saw what she had been doing.

"I guess we had better dig out the old camping stuff," he said ruefully.

He gave her a quick hug. "What are you doing?" he asked. "we didn't go to sleep until nearly one, and it's way too early to be up."

"I know," Irma replied shakily. She felt close to tears. "But I couldn't sleep. I kept thinking about those poor people on the plane. I hope everything comes back on soon."

By one in the afternoon, there were still no lights and no traffic had passed. It was eerily quiet, the only sound that of the birds singing and the creak of their rocking chairs as they sipped their lunchtime tea.

Finally, Tony got to his feet decisively. "Let's go over to the Johnson's and see if they've heard anything."

Irma nodded. "Good idea, dear. You go start the car and I'll comb my hair and be ready in five minutes".

Five minutes later she came out onto the porch and found Tony staring under the hood of her car.

"It won't start." He scratched his head and then replaced the battered baseball cap he wore. "I tried the pickup, your car, even the lawnmower…none of them will start. What in hell is going on?"

"Language, dear." She admonished him coming down the steps.

He smiled shakily. "How do you feel about a walk, Mother? Think these old bones can make a mile to the Dennis's?"

"I thought we were going to the Johnson's?"

"That was my first thought, but if we walk across the field, the Dennis's are closer." He slammed the hood shut and reached for her hand. "Oh, and I'd change my shoes if I were you. Those sandals aren't going to get you far."

An hour later they were seated in Flora Dennis' kitchen sipping warm beer.

"Sorry, folks", Flora said as she placed a tray of cold cuts and cheese on the table. "No fridge, so everything is warm. We need to eat this meat. It won't last long."

Irma laughed, helped herself to a piece of ham and folded it onto a cracker. "At least the beer won't go bad. You can always put it in the creek to keep cool."

"Have you heard anything?" Tony asked his neighbour. "We can't even go to town and ask because none of our vehicles will start."

"Barry's riding his bike down to the school", Flora nodded. "Our cars don't start either, and the mail truck didn't show up this morning. Hopefully, there will be someone there who knows what's going on."

Tony nodded. The school was a community hall and the centre for information in the district.

"Where's Ervin?" Tony looked around the kitchen. As usual, dishes and the detritus of daily living were piled on the counter and the floor needed a good cleaning. With five children, Flora couldn't always keep up with all the housework. She just smiled cheerfully and said it was more important to have happy kids than a spotless house.

"He's out in the old barn." Flora waved her hand vaguely indicating the direction, "He's looking to see if we have any propane for the camp stove." She shrugged her broad shoulders. "We need to feed the brood, even without an electric range. Plus, I want to cook up as much of our meat as possible before it goes bad."

"So, are you thinking this will last a long time?" the old man asked.

"Who knows, but I don't want to lose all my meat. The freezer will keep it for a few days but better safe than sorry."

Tony and Irma glanced nervously at each other. Each knew what the other was thinking. In the August heat it would be hard to keep things fresh for very long.

'We'd better get home." Tony stood as he swallowed the final mouthful of beer. "We need to look for more candles and some flashlights in case we need them tonight."

"Might as well wait until Barry comes back from the school," came a booming voice from the kitchen door. "At least we might get an idea of how widespread this power outage is. Have another beer, Tony."

"Yes, you're right." Tony sat down and placed his cap on the table in front of him. "No hurry, I guess. It doesn't get dark until late." He accepted another bottle of beer and leaned back in the chair.

Ervin sat down, popped a beer, and took a small boy onto his lap.

"So, what did we find in the barn, Brent? Anything useful?"

For the next few minutes, they examined the contents of a wooden box. A small propane container, a flashlight and a battered coffee pot.

"All useful things." Ervin boomed. "Good thing I'm a packrat, hey Flora?"

She smiled back at him and lifted their baby from a crib in the corner of the cluttered kitchen. "Yep, good thing." She gave Irma a wink. "What are you gonna do, hey Irma?"

"You want to hold the baby." She handed the bundle over. "I don't think you've seen her yet, have you?"

Eagerly, Irma reached for the baby girl. "No, I haven't seen her. What's her name?"

"Bella." Flora draped a towel over her neighbour's shoulder. "Never know when you might need that. I wanted Isabella," she continued, "but all our kids have 'B' names, so we compromised."

"That's nice." Irma gently stroked the soft hair that curled around the tiny ears. "I've only seen our grandson once."

"Jason has a kid?" Ervin asked.

Tony answered for his distracted wife. "Yes, Jack's about a year old now. You'd think they lived in Timbuktu instead of only 150 kilometres away in Prince George."

"They're busy." Irma defended her son. "He's got that new job and his wife is a teacher. It's not that easy to get away."

While they were talking, fourteen-year-old Barry returned from his exploration journey. His face was red from exertion as he rushed into the kitchen demanding water and something to eat.

"I'm starved", he declared. "It's a long ride to school on a bike".

Tony surveyed the lanky teenager but refrained from mentioning his own school days when he walked the five miles each way in all kinds of weather. *And uphill both ways* he chuckled to himself. That was a long time ago, and in his opinion, today's kids were too soft.

"So, what did you find out?" his parents watched him stuff the remaining ham and cheese into his hungry mouth. "Slow down," his mom admonished him. "You won't starve in the next two minutes. Was anybody there?"

"Yep, lots of people. Everybody wants to know what's going on and how long before it's fixed."

"And…."

The boy swallowed. "Nobody knows. Somebody said there was a bomb went off somewhere and somebody else said aliens were attacking...but nobody knows for sure."

"Was anybody from the power company there?" asked his mother anxiously. Both of his explanations were beneath consideration in her opinion.

"Nope, but Mr. Taylor the principal, said he had seen someone from town passing on a bike and he said all the power is out there too. Phones don't work and cars don't run. Tim's dad said there was a big accident on the highway at about ten o'clock. All the cars just quit. It's a mess!"

"That's when we saw the plane crash."

The four adults glanced at each other. What was going on? This sounded like more than a regular power outage. The teenager was nonchalant about the whole affair. To him, it seemed like a movie or TV show. To the older people, it was all too real.

"We'd better go, Mother." Tony stood up and Irma handed the baby back to her mother.

"You take care of that little one," she told her.

Flora grinned and patted her husband's hand. "We'll be fine." She answered. "We're tough, aren't we Ervin?"

Someone banging on the door brought Monica jumping to her feet. For a moment she gazed around in confusion. The sun had barely shown itself above the horizon and the apartment was bathed in a dim, gray light.

Her head cleared and she hastily made her way to the door. She could hear Jack starting to wail.

She reached for the lock, then hesitated. "Who is it?" she hated that she sounded so tentative.

"It's me. Open the door."

Hearing Jason's voice, she quickly disengaged the lock and pulled the door open. "Oh, wait a minute. I forgot the chain is on."

The door swung open and she fell into her husband's arms. For a moment they stood wrapped together, silent.

Monica stepped back first. "I need to get Jack." The baby's cries were getting louder. "You look awful. Go sit down."

He turned and secured the door before moving slowly towards the kitchen. "What do we have to drink?" he asked. "Any bottled water, or juice?"

He opened the dark refrigerator and surveyed its contents. Besides baby formula, there was some ginger ale and half a jug of water. He poured some of the water into a glass and sat down just as Monica returned with Jack in her arms.

She set the baby in his high chair with a dish of dry cereal and began to prepare his formula.

"So, what happened?" she asked.

Wearily he dropped his head into his hand. "Nobody has a clue." He said. "It's kind of a war zone out there. Everybody is trying to help where they can, but there's no way to contact each other. We didn't see any police or fire trucks. One of the guys I was walking with took off to the nearest police station, but I never saw him again."

He raised haunted eyes to hers. "It's scary, Monica. No phones, no vehicles, no central authority. And look at us. Up here, we have no water and the only way out is down ten flights of stairs."

"You need to sleep." She said firmly as she settled Jack for his morning bottle. "I'm sure they will have this fixed soon, and in the meantime, we have a case of water in the closet, and enough formula for a few days."

"But don't you see." He leaned forward and grasped both hands in hers. "We can't sleep. Everybody is going to be swarming the grocery stores for supplies and if we wait a day there won't be anything left. We need to get out there right away."

"Even if that's true, and this lasts more than a few days," Monica said, "How will we get anything up here? We have a baby to carry, and, as you said, it's ten stories."

He released her hands and took a sip of his water. "I thought of that. We can get a grocery cart at the store and leave everything we can't carry in the car. I'll carry Jack on my back, so each of us will have two free hands. It'll be a long walk, but we're both fit and can do it."

"Okay," she nodded. "you're right we can do it. But we should also check on Mrs. Scully next door. There's no way she can walk down those stairs. I'll bet she's scared out of her mind right now."

He nodded. "Everybody's scared. Power outages are one thing, but all the phones, all the motors, everything we depend on, has stopped." He hesitated a moment, then said, "How much cash do we have?

Monica looked at him blankly. "Cash?"

"Yeah, you know. That crinkly stuff that you spend when all the ATM machines or Visa terminals don't work."

"I don't know. Maybe a hundred dollars if we empty Jack's piggy bank?"

He drained his glass then stood up. "We'd better look. Empty your purse, then I'll check all our change while you go find out if Mrs. Scully is okay. Maybe she could even watch Jack while we go to the store."

As she stepped out into the hall he called after her, "And ask her if she has any cash."

When the apartment door closed behind her, Monica leaned against the wall. Tears filled her eyes. Her shoulders sagged, then with a determined look, she stood up to her full five feet ten-inch height and made her way to apartment 1012.

The door opened a fraction in response to her knock. Frightened eyes looked up at her, then a smile as the older woman recognized her neighbour.

"Oh, Monica." Mrs. Scully released the safety chain and threw open the door. "I've been so scared. What's happening?"

The two women hugged, Monica bending almost in half to reach the tiny person in front of her.

"I don't know what's happening either." She responded. "Jason went out last night to help and he just came back. Nobody knows what happened, just that everything electrical has stopped."

"Come and sit down." Monica followed the grey head into the kitchen. "I was watching the traffic last night, and it was awful. I tried to call you, but my phone didn't work, and I was too scared to go into the dark hall, so I've just been sitting here worrying."

"Do you want a glass of juice or anything? Of course, there is no coffee." She finally came to the end of her frantic speech and looked expectantly at her guest.

"No, nothing," Monica answered. "I just came over to see if you are all right. And to ask you if you will watch the baby while Jason and I go out to try to get some supplies."

"Well, I'm fine now that I have seen a friendly face. It was pretty scary in here all alone last night. Do you think this might go on for a while? What kind of supplies?" she paused for breath. "And of course I'll watch Jack. You know I love to have him. Should I come over to your place, or will you bring him here?"

Monica smiled. "Why don't you come over to our place? All Jack's stuff is there and it's easier that way. If you don't mind."

"By the way," she continued before the older woman could break in, "Do you have any cash in the house? Our credit cards won't work. Of course, it'll just be a loan until things are back to normal."

"Sure I do." Mrs. Scully reached for her purse. "How much do you need?"

"As much as you have," Monica answered. "We don't know what will be available, or how long we need to prepare for."

To her surprise, Mrs. Scully handed her a roll of bills as thick around as her wrist. Monica loosened the rubber band that held it together and gasped.

"Do you always carry around a roll of hundred dollar bills?"

"No, not always. But I just got my pension cheque, and I like to keep cash on hand." She snapped her purse shut and stood up. "You never know what'll happen, do you?"

Monica was still shaking her head when she unlocked her own apartment and ushered Mrs. Scully inside. The baby crowed at the sight of his favourite baby sitter. Jason looked up from the cereal he was eating and gave them a strained smile.

"Thank you for coming, Mrs. Scully." He reached over and gave her a quick hug. "Monica, you had better eat something. We don't know how long we'll be gone."

"Don't you worry," The older woman lifted Jack from his high chair. "We'll be just fine, won't we Jackie? You take as long as you need and be careful. People get crazy when they're scared."

CHAPTER THREE

Walking home in the late afternoon, Tony felt a little woozy. He wasn't used to drinking beer in the middle of the day. It was hours until sunset and still hot. Irma held his arm for their mutual support.

"What do you suppose really happened?" she asked him. "It's so weird that everything should stop working."

"I don't know," he shrugged and clutched her arm a little tighter as he stumbled a bit on the gravel. "but I do know that we are lucky to have a propane stove and the old well. I don't know what they will do in a city apartment if this lasts more than a few days."

Irma nodded. "I'm worried about Jason and Monica," she confided. "I wish we had some way to reach them."

"They'll be fine. I'm sure this will be over soon and they'll call."

But he was worried too. As they strolled down their own driveway he glanced towards the old well. It had been covered up for years. He wondered if there was water in it, and how deep it went. Did he even have a bucket to carry water? Back when he had sold most of the farm to a developer it had seemed like a good idea to go on the communal water system. Now he wondered.

He sighed, but smiled at his concerned wife. "Let's have a nap" he suggested. "Then we can sit and make a plan. We were up way too early and then this long walk. I can't even think right now."

"Good idea." She smiled back bravely. "And when we wake up, I'll start emptying the freezer. If we can get some water for cooking" she added.

It was the next afternoon before Tony uncovered the well and peered into its depths. "Looks like there's water down there," he muttered to himself.

"What're you doin'?" the voice came from above him and he looked up, startled.

"Geez, Sam. I nearly fell in."

His neighbor sat astride his favourite horse, grinning widely. "Just thought I'd come over and see how things were here." He slid down and landed with a slight groan. "Damn, I'm not as young as I used to be."

"None of us are." Tony stood up and shook his neighbour's hand. "Just checkin' to see if I can hook up the old well until the power comes on."

Sam looked into the black hole. "How long since that old pump has worked?" He asked. "It seems that all motors are out of commission. Did you hear about the accidents on the highway the other night?"

"Yeah," he nodded. "We walked over to the Dennis's yesterday and their boy told us there had been a crash, but he didn't know any details."

"Everything quit!" Sam's wrinkled forehead furrowed. "Everything. I've got two hundred milking cows and no machines. Stella and I were out at four this morning trying to milk by hand, but we couldn't do more than fifty before our hands gave up." He looked down at his arthritic hands.

"And that kid who is supposed to help didn't show up." He turned away and stroked the horse's nose. "Can't blame him, I suppose. No car, and he's probably never had to walk more than a block in his life. And the old lady is almost as useless as he is."

Tony winced. He had called Irma the old lady once and regretted it for a week.

"So, what about the well?" Sam turned back and his voice became brisk. "You might have to pull the water up with a bucket."

Tony scratched his face. The two days of whiskers were itchy and he hated all the grey that was showing up. Somehow it seemed worse than the white in his hair.

"Thing is," he said. "It's an artesian well. Worked for a hundred years without a pump. All I have to do is go down there and reconnect the pipe."

"How you gonna do that? It's fifty feet deep."

Tony looked thoughtful. "If I can find a fifty foot rope, we can tie it to the horse and you can let me down there. Then I can hook it up and the horse can pull me back up."

"Might work." Sam patted the horse again. "What do you think, Star?"

"Just don't tell Irma what we're doing." Tony warned. "She'll think I'm too old and worry herself sick. But we need water."

An hour later he was balanced on a board they had lowered into the well, a flashlight shining on the water a mere six inches below him. Far above him Sam's worried face showed as a black spot against a tiny circle of light.

He pointed his flashlight at the crumbling wall of dirt and began scanning the area. After what seemed like an eternity he was finally rewarded with a flash of metal. One pipe poked out of the ground. He knew that led to the house, put there many years before by his grandfather. Water bubbled from a second pipe that poked up from the pool below him. An artesian well ran constantly, so by forcing the water into the pipe, gravity would feed it into the house. Carefully he attached the hose he had brought from the shop to both pipes, wrapping duct tape around the joints. It leaked a bit, but hopefully it would hold until the community water came back on.

He tugged on the rope and called. "Okay, Sam. Pull me up."

Stepping out onto the grass he said confidently, "Now all I have to do is turn the spigot that channelled the water, and it should work."

From the kitchen window, Irma saw the two men walking towards her. The horse ambled between them and Tony was carrying a length of rope. "Now what're they up to?" she wondered.

She was washing dishes in lukewarm water, she had carried from the creek. "Like the dark ages."

Well, at least they had propane so she could heat it, but it got cold way too fast. She sighed, then looked up as Tony rapped on the kitchen window.

"What?" she pushed against the old fashioned panes and the window slid open.

"Try the tap."

Confused she looked down at the cast iron sink. "The tap? Why?"

"just turn it on." Tony grinned at her.

Water gushed out. "What did you do?" she almost squealed in delight.

"Wait, we're coming in." They disappeared around the corner of the house, then she heard the back door open.

"We hooked up the old well." Tony gave her a quick hug. "Sam and his horse came at just the right time."

"It'll only be cold water, and it's only in the kitchen." He explained further. "But we can flush the toilet with buckets, and I can shave."

Irma looked at him suspiciously. "Did you climb down that dangerous old well?" she demanded. "You could have been killed."

"Well, I wasn't. Was I Sam?" Sam grinned back at him. "And now you can offer our guest some tea."

"No, no, I have to get home. Stella will be worried. She hates to be alone and besides I'm going to try to milk a few more cows tonight."

"I wish I could help you," Tony said. "But I've never milked a cow in my life. We were grain and beef farmers."

"Oh, I guess we'll manage for a few days." The two men shook hands, Sam kissed Irma on the cheek, then left for home. The couple stepped out onto the porch and watched the horse disappear through the gate.

"I never liked that man." Irma turned to go back into the house. "But he came along at the right time today. Thank goodness we've got water I don't have to carry. Wonderful!"

"He's not so bad," Tony followed her into the kitchen. "His farm is one of the best in the province. He and his wife seem to work twenty-four hours a day keeping it up."

Irma glanced in his direction and shook her head slightly.

"What?"

"Nothing. Nothing at all. Just sometimes women see what men miss, that's all." And she busied herself making tea for the two of them.

CHAPTER FOUR

The leaves were starting to turn colour when Tony and Irma were interrupted one afternoon by a young RCMP officer on a horse.

He dismounted and made his way across the garden, stepping carefully between the rows.

"Any news?" Tony asked eagerly. "Do we know when this will end?"

The young man shook his head. "Only rumours," he answered, clutching his hat in his hands. "But police stations across the country are trying to keep in touch by sending riders on bicycles and horseback. The story seems to be that someone set off some kind of bomb that disrupted power grids all across the country".

"Do we know who that someone might have been?" asked Irma, concern knotting her forehead.

The officer sighed. "No, but of course everybody puts the blame on the Middle East. Maybe it was Syria, maybe it was Iraq or even Iran. North Korea was mentioned, but nobody thinks they have the know-how to do something on this scale."

"What about in town?" Tony asked. "We have a garden, but I bet things are getting a little tense there."

"The Red Cross set up food stations and are telling people to come to shelters if they have to. But with no way to get new supplies in, they're running out of stuff too. The stores are getting emptied out. And of course, it's all word of mouth," he added miserably. "No real way to communicate."

Tony looked thoughtful. "We were thinking of going into town to see if we could stock up on essentials," he told the cop. "Guess that would be kind of useless."

"I wouldn't bother." The young man shook his head. "Everything's cleaned out, and people are getting pretty aggressive. Mostly they're scared. Some are packing up and going south. Guess they figure it'll be warmer in the winter."

He was still shaking his head as he rode away. His back slumped when he thought they were no longer watching. Obviously, he was as shaken as they were, but he had a job to do and he was doing it to the best of his ability.

The old couple linked hands as they watched the horse disappear up the driveway.

"Let's take another look around and make sure we got all we could." Irma led the way up and down the empty rows. She shivered in the late afternoon sunshine.

"The winds up," Tony observed and bent to pull one lonely carrot that had been left behind. He wiped the dirt on his denim overalls and absently began to chew. "And the leaves are changing. It's going to be getting cold pretty soon."

Irma glanced at the nearby forest. "Thank goodness for propane stoves." She observed. "We were able to can most of the vegetables. All our meat from the freezer has been cooked and packed in brine. We won't run out of food for a while."

Tony shook his head ruefully, "Too bad we didn't keep a root cellar like on the farm. If we have no way to heat the garage, all of it will freeze anyway."

Irma turned frightened eyes to him. "Oh surely it will be fixed before winter" she exclaimed. "It's not so bad in the summer when it's light until ten o'clock, but what will happen if the power is still out in December?"

She began to cry, tears dripping down her wrinkled cheeks and blurring the dim blue eyes even more.

"And where are Jason and Monica?" sobs shook her small body. "We haven't heard a word from them and there is no way they could stay in an apartment with no heat and no electricity."

All her fears had been released by one small tear.

"They have the baby. What are they feeding him? Why hasn't he sent some kind of message?"

"Now now, Mother," Tony comforted her. He held her close against him and patted her back. Truth be told, he was as frightened as she, but men of his generation were not allowed to show tears or weakness. His job was to keep her safe and worry free.

He hugged her harder so she couldn't see the misery on his face. "I'm sure he is okay," he said. "You know it's over a hundred miles and there's no quick way to send a message."

"Jim's son came from the city on a bike", she countered. "He told us how bad it is…all the stores are empty and closed. No elevators, so people are trapped on the higher floors. Fire hydrants don't work, and even if they did, the trucks don't start, so fires are starting everywhere and burning out of control."

She drew a shaky breath. "We're lucky, we can start the barbecue or light a fire in the fireplace, but what do you do if you are on the tenth floor and have no heat? What if this power outage lasts? People will die."

"I know," he patted her back comfortingly. "We can only wait and hope he finds a way to get home."

"Maybe we could go find him." Excitement lit up her features as she pulled out of his embrace. "We have bicycles and could go to the city."

Tony laughed softly. "Oh Mother, do you know how long it would take to get there? We're way too old to spend a week or more on a bike. And anyway, I'm sure he will make his way to us, and if we weren't here to meet him, think how he would worry. More than we are now, I'll bet. They're young and will come when they can".

"I'm sorry." She straightened her back resolutely. "It's not like me to start blubbering like that, is it? I know you are just as worried."

"Let's start thinking about where we can store the canned food so it doesn't freeze. Come on, Mother. It's tea time."

As they walked towards the house, both pretending to smile, Irma wondered just how much longer their tea would last.

Monica gazed down to where cars still littered the street. Some of them had tires missing and glass glittered on the hoods. Doors hung open like gaping mouths. A few people moved slowly between them, looking for anything of value that might be exchanged for food.

She sighed and turned away from the window. Mrs. Scully looked up from her needlework and smiled. "Don't worry, sweetheart. I'm sure that someone is working on getting things fixed."

"I sure hope so." Monica joined her on the couch. "All the food that we managed to get that first week is nearly gone. And I'd kill for a shower."

The older woman patted her hand. "Maybe Jason will bring us some news today."

"I should have gone with him." Monica stood up and began to pace around the small living room. "I'm going crazy in here." She stopped pacing and smiled at her guest. "Thank goodness you are here, Mrs. Scully, or I really would go crazy. And without your money, we would be in even worse straits."

"Now, now, dear. I've told you a million times to call me Myrna. And thank you for the kind words, but sometimes I wonder if I'm not just an unnecessary burden. You might have left and gone somewhere safer if not for me."

"Don't be silly." Monica looked horrified. "Without you to watch Jack and keep me company, we would be worse off."

"Oh, here's Jason." She broke off as the key turned in the lock.

"Damn that chain." He muttered as the door came to a halt after opening only a few inches.

Monica pulled the chain out of its slot. "You know we have to keep it on," she admonished him. "It might not keep anybody out if they were determined, but at least it would slow them down."

"I know. I know. It's just not our usual way of living." He hoisted a case of water into the apartment, and then went back for the bag he had left outside the door. "This is the last of our supplies." He told her. "The car is empty now."

"Is there any news out there?" Myrna Scully asked.

"Nothing." Jason raised his eyes to meet his wife's. There was no hope in them. For a moment she noted how long his beard was, and how it matched his auburn hair. She stepped into his arms and for a moment they felt like they were alone.

When they broke apart, Mrs. Scully was giving all her attention to the embroidery hoop she held.

"You should leave." She told them, her voice strong. "Pretty soon it will be winter and with no food, or heat, this apartment is a trap."

"We can go to my parents," Jason answered slowly. "If we take the food we have left, we can get water from the river. It's only a hundred miles. We can do it in a week or so."

"You should go." The older woman stood up and grasped their hands. "You have to think of Jack."

"We wouldn't go without you." Monica squeezed the old hand.

"Me!" She released their hands. "I'm eighty-five years old! I can't even walk down the stairs to the street, let alone a hundred miles or more."

"No, no. You leave me that case of water and we'll tell Nestor down the hall that I'm here. He'll bring any food he finds to share with me. I'll be okay."

"We are not leaving you here alone." Jason touched her shoulder. "Nestor is gone. He told me he was going to try to get further south before winter. Don't worry, we'll think of something."

Lying in the dark a few hours later, Jason and Monica discussed their plan.

"We can carry her down the stairs," Jason said. "We have the baby's stroller"

"I don't think she'd fit in a stroller." Monica countered. "She's tiny, but not that tiny. And what about Jack?"

"We'll carry Jack on our backs. If we have the stroller we can also carry some supplies and whatever you can't bear to leave behind, like our wedding picture."

"Or," his voice became thoughtful. "What if I take the wheels off the stroller and build some kind of wagon? It'd be a rough ride, but we can line it with blankets. Then we can carry more diapers and baby supplies too."

The next morning, Monica could hardly wait to tell Myrna their plan. They were up early and Jason went into the car park to find materials for the wagon. She moved around the apartment, choosing what they would need for their long walk.

"It's funny," she told the baby. "We needed so much stuff and now I find we can live with some water and food and a few diapers." The baby chortled in reply and she smiled at him.

"I wonder where Myrna is." She kept up the one-sided conversation. "Usually she comes over by now. It must be hard to be all alone and so worried. I hope we have alleviated some of that for her."

At noon, Jason came upstairs for some lunch. He glanced around the apartment. "Where's Mrs. Scully?" he asked.

"I don't know." Monica set a bowl of soup in front of him. "Eat up, that's the last can. I'll run over and tell her that lunch is ready."

She was back in a few minutes, tears rolling down her cheeks. She handed him a folded piece of paper then sat down heavily beside him.

Slowly he straightened the paper and read the note that had been left for them.

"Dear Monica and Jason" it started. *"I'm eighty five years old and have lived a good life. While I appreciate that you want to help me, it is my turn to help you, by removing myself from the equation. I have some old sleeping pills left over, enough to put me to sleep forever. Please don't mourn me, but take Jack and go somewhere safe. Thank you for all you have done to make an old lady happy. All my love, Myrna."*

He put his arm around his sobbing wife and pulled her chair closer. "She didn't want to burden us."

"She was no burden." Monica buried her head in his shoulder. "Ever since my parents died I've thought of her as an extra grandparent."

"I know." He pulled her closer. "But now she would want us to get on with it. The wagon is ready, so I think we should get out of here as soon as possible while the weather is still okay. In another few days, it could be snowing."

She sat up and wiped her eyes with her sleeve. "Should we just leave her there?"

"Where would we take her?" he asked reasonably. "She chose to die in her home and I'm sure that there are lots of elderly people who have taken the same way out. She knows we will miss her, and that has to be what we remember."

Monica nodded and wiped her eyes. "You go down and finish the wagon. I'm just about ready to go. Before we leave, maybe we could go in and say goodbye to our good old friend."

CHAPTER FIVE

September was well on its way, and still, there was no power, no telephone and worst of all, no car. Irma tried not to think of the winter to come, but in spite of herself, worry kept rearing its ugly head.

With no motorized equipment, they were turning over the garden soil with spades. It was hard work and Tony straightened up, putting a hand on his lower back and grimacing.

"I sure miss the rotor tiller." He told his wife. "I'd forgotten how...." his voice trailed away. Irma glanced up. He was staring intently down the driveway.

"What is it?" She straightened up also and glanced towards the gate.

The sun was shining brightly, causing a glare on her glasses so she had to squint to see the two figures making their way towards them. A man and a woman, both carrying backpacks. The man had a red beard and his hair stood up in wild disarray. His companion seemed to have trouble keeping up.

But wait! Irma started towards the couple. Something about them was familiar. The way they walked, the shape of their bodies. She took a few steps toward them.

And realized the man was carrying on his back, not a pack, but a baby.

Irma and Tony began to run, laughing and crying at the same time.

The two couples, young and old, met near the front porch.

"Oh, Jason!" the mother cried. "You made it! You came!"

For a moment the four of them stood in a tight circle, arms around each other's shoulders. Their bodies shook and tears came. Even Tony let emotion rule the moment. His son was home.

After a moment, they pulled apart.

"How…"

"We're so…"

"It's so good…"

"Wait, Wait!" Irma held up her hand to stop them all talking at once. "We want to know everything, but first the most important thing."

She walked behind her son and tenderly loosened the straps that were holding the baby in place. He peered at her curiously with his bright blue eyes. The soother in his mouth moved in and out as he sucked frantically.

"Come on, little Jack. Come to your grandma." He came easily into her arms, still gazing intently at the unfamiliar face. "Oh Monica," she murmured. "He's so beautiful."

"And hungry," said his mother. "We haven't had any food for him since yesterday."

"Yesterday! You haven't eaten since yesterday? Why didn't you say so? We have cereal and some powdered milk. Come in the house and rest." Irma took her daughter-in-law's arm. "We've been so worried about you," she confided. "I am so glad you are here and safe."

The two women were almost at the door when they realized their husbands weren't with them.

"Come on, Jason. You need something to eat too."

"We'll be along in a minute, Mom," Tony said in a quiet voice. "You go into the house and look after little Jack."

Something in his tone made Irma turn back. The men were standing very still and watching something in the driveway.

"What is it?" she asked.

Jason's teeth shone through the tangled red beard as he grinned at her. "Nothing, Mom. There were a couple of boys behind us on the road, and I want to make sure they kept going."

"They might be hungry too." She answered. "If they come in, we'll feed them."

The door closed a little too loudly behind her. Tony grinned at his son. "She's a little testy at the moment, Son. It's been a long few weeks." He gave him a quick squeeze and was surprised at how much taller the boy was all of a sudden. Or maybe he had always been this tall, but hugs had been so few and far between, he hadn't noticed.

His voice lowered as he asked, "So what's with these boys? Should we be worried?"

"They were following us for the past couple of days," Jason answered. "They never got too close, but maybe they were waiting for the right moment. Monica and I were pretty careful where we stopped and one of us stayed awake all the time to watch the baby." He paused. "Do you still have those hunting rifles around?"

"Yeah, they're in the upstairs closet. I started to notice a few shady characters eying up the garden, so to be on the safe side, I moved them out of the safe, along with some ammunition a few days ago."

He sighed heavily. "I never thought I'd see the day I had to have a loaded gun in my house."

"Let's just hope we don't have to use it," his son replied. "I don't see the boys now, and I'm starving, so let's go in. We can keep an eye out for them."

Sitting at the familiar table, eating a quickly assembled meal of soup and sandwiches, Jason let himself relax. He gazed around. Nothing had changed really. There was a new propane stove and the refrigerator had been replaced, but the old chrome table with its matching chairs was pushed up against the same flowered wallpaper. The cast iron sink and the old-fashioned faucets set into the speckled counter were the same. In the corner where the stairs began, the linoleum was worn down to the wood. He knew the only bathroom and the three bedrooms up there had never been updated. The wind probably whistled through the same cracks in the window frames. Above that, there was the attic where he had played as a boy. It was always warm up there, he remembered, partly because of the brick chimney that formed its centre.

The old dog watched him from his rumpled bed under the window. He knew that under that bed was a trap door that led to a damp crawl space.

Tony grinned. "Not much changed, hey, son?"

"Nope." Jason leaned back in his chair. "It's just like I always remember." He nodded towards the corner. "Are you still using that old root cellar?"

"It's pretty much fallen in." His father replied thoughtfully. "I should have had it dug down years ago but it was never at the top of my list." He shrugged. "And then with only the two of us and not knowing how long we'd be here…" His voice trailed off.

Jason concentrated on his soup for a moment, then lifted his eyes to meet those of his Dad's. "I know I didn't come home often enough." He lowered his eyes. "But I never thought the day would come when you wouldn't be here waiting. Kind of like a really long school bus ride."

"You're here now." Irma placed a cup of weak coffee at his elbow. "And now I can sleep at night."

"You're right, Mom." He nodded and reached over to touch her hand. "We have to be prepared in case this 'incident' goes on." He laughed. "That's what the Red Cross and the police were calling it. An 'incident', like people weren't dying all around us."

Tony stood up. "Let's take our coffee outside, Jason. I want to see where those boys went. We can discuss the situation later."

Grabbing their cups, the two men returned to the front porch. There was no sign of anybody in the drive, so they sat down to wait.

Inside the house, Irma sent her daughter-in-law upstairs with the baby in her arms. Quickly and efficiently she cleaned the remains of the meal from the counters. It was crucial to keep everything in its place so when darkness fell, there was nothing to trip them up.

Her forehead furrowed as she counted the remaining cans and dry goods in the pantry. "We'll have to cut back on using soup for quick meals," she mused to herself. They won't go bad as long as we can keep them from freezing. And we really should use up the fresh food first." Luckily, they had a bumper harvest of potatoes and carrots from the garden "And there are two boxes of cereal the baby can have," she continued to muse. "A little flour and there's still two big bags of sugar and a box of powdered milk."

"Who are you talking to, Mom?" Monica's voice startled her so much, she jumped, then laughed.

"Sorry," she chuckled. "I'm so used to being alone you startled me. I was talking to myself"

The younger woman crossed the kitchen floor and gave her a quick hug. "Well, you don't have to talk to yourself any longer. I'm here to help." She glanced into the nearly empty pantry, then at the neat kitchen. She noted the gas lantern and candles on the table and the bucket of water on the corner of the counter. A basin was in the sink, holding the lunch dishes to be washed.

"It looks like you're pretty organized", she observed.

"Yes, we are lucky." Her mother-in-law answered. "We have lots of propane for the stove, so we can cook and heat water. Dad opened up the old well and hooked it up, so we have cold water to the kitchen sink." She indicated the pail of water. "That's used water for flushing the toilet " She opened the door to the attached garage so Monica could admire the jars of vegetables and meat she had preserved.

"The garden kept growing, so we have canned peas and beans, and there are lots of potatoes and carrots." Monica nodded in appreciation.

"I canned all the meat from the freezer." Irma laughed. "Luckily I still had all my old canning jars. I hadn't used them in years, but couldn't bear to throw them away. And my old cookbooks reminded me how to preserve foods. We had lots of cabbage too, so I used all the salt I could find to start some sauerkraut. Not really an Italian dish," she smiled ruefully. "But it's one of the most nutritious meals you can have."

Monica's nose wrinkled. She wasn't sure about sauerkraut.

"There were advantages to growing up on a farm. At least we know how to survive these days." Irma's eyes filled. "Do you know what happened?" she asked shakily. "All of a sudden life stopped, and nobody has any idea why. There's just a bunch of silly rumours."

"I think we have heard the same rumours", Monica gave her another squeeze around the shoulders." aliens, North Korean bombs, Russian weather disruptors…who knows what really happened. All we can hope is that it will be fixed before winter."

Irma shook her head. "All my work canning the food won't be worth anything if it all freezes."

She turned decisively and marched to the stove. "Nothing we can do about that now. Let's just have a nice cup of tea and a visit. Later we can worry about winter and heat and all that. Right now, I want to hear all about your trek to get here, and how little Jack is doing."

CHAPTER SIX

On the front porch, Tony and Jason sipped the last two bottles of beer. Tony had a twenty-two lying casually across his lap.

"I've been saving these for a special occasion." Tony raised his bottle in a salute to his son. "And I guess this is as special as it gets."

His smile faded as he gazed across the front yard. The cars still sat in the driveway. There was no sound of traffic going by. No radio playing in the background. The forest that he had loved all his life now looked dark and threatening. "Truth to tell, son, I'm glad you're here for a number of reasons."

Jason started to interrupt, but Tony held up his hand to stop any protests. "I'm happy you are safe and I get to tell you how worried we were, and how much we..." he hesitated, trying to find words that he was not accustomed to saying out loud.

"How much I love you." He glanced up, uncertain how his words would be received. These words he hadn't said to his son, since he was a baby.

Jason had his head down, staring at his half-full beer bottle. "Thanks, Dad. That means a lot." He looked up and Tony saw that he had tears in his eyes. "I had a lot of time to think in the last couple of weeks, locked up in an apartment, and then walking for days. I remembered how much fun I had here when I was growing up, and how I always felt safe and loved. You don't have to say it, because I always knew it.

And Dad," their eyes met momentarily, "I love you too. And now that we have that out of the way, no more mushy stuff. It looks like we have a lot of more important things to worry about."

His voice dropped to a whisper, "Those two boys who were following us are in the driveway. No! Don't look." Tony's head instinctively turned towards the road. "They're hiding behind the shed."

"They're probably as hungry as you were," Tony said softly. "Why don't we call them over and see what they want. How old do you think they are?"

"Probably about fifteen." Jason stood up and raised his voice. "Hey, you boys," he shouted. "Why don't you come and say hello instead of hiding like a couple of criminals?"

"Come over here." Tony joined in. "I'll bet you're hungry."

The door behind them opened and Irma stuck her head out. "Who are you shouting at?" she demanded. "The baby's sleeping."

"Or he was," as a wail rose behind her.

"It's those boys." Jason pointed. "We want them to come in and tell us what they want instead of sneaking around."

Irma stepped out and stood behind Tony. "Do you think they want to steal something?"

"No, I think they are hungry. Come in, Boys," he shouted. "Hot soup on the table in five minutes." He stood up and set the gun to one side.

Slowly, two lanky forms appeared from behind the shed. One of the boys was blond, and the other was dark, but both were dirty and very thin. Hesitantly, with their hands held in front of them, they approached the three people at the front door of the farmhouse.

Irma watched them come with a compassionate look in her eyes. She stepped forward and held out her arms as if to hug them.

"Come on, boys." She encouraged. "You don't want to hurt anyone do you?"

Tony spoke more gruffly. "What do you want?" He stressed the word do. "Are you hungry?"
They both nodded diffidently.

"Well, come on then. Mother, why don't you bring something out here for them. They both look too dirty to eat in the house."

Four pairs of concerned eyes watched as the two scruffy boys wolfed down a can of soup and a loaf of Irma's fresh bread. Nobody spoke, the boys because they were busy chewing and swallowing, and the adults because they were waiting to hear their story.

Finally, after a last mouthful of water, their 'guests' put down their spoons and leaned back in their chairs.

"Thank you." Said the blond boy. "I don't know when I have been so hungry."

"Me too." His darker companion agreed. "I'm sorry we were so rude, but I couldn't seem to stop."

Irma stood and began to clear the dishes from the picnic table. "That's okay, boys. We understand." She was clearly disturbed by their appearance. They were both so thin that she felt sure their dirty jeans were going to fall right off. She tried not to wrinkle her nose as she leaned closer to pick up the empty bread dish. They both needed a good bath too.

Jason cleared his throat. "Why were you following us?" he asked brusquely.

"We thought you might have some food." The blond boy admitted. "And then we saw you didn't, so we just stayed with you because we had no place else to go."

Standing behind him, Irma patted his shoulder. "It's okay," she said softly. "Where are your families? And we should know what to call you. I'm Mrs. Baldini and that's my husband," indicating Tony with a nod. "And that's my son Jason and his wife Monica. They are the ones you scared so badly by following them."

"I'm Tom. And this is my friend Adnan." Adnan ducked his head shyly. "And we're really sorry for scaring you. We're neighbours and we both thought if we went into the country, the power might be on and things might be better."

Tears began to fill his eyes, but he shook them away with an obvious effort. "There's no food left in our houses and we both eat a lot, so we told our moms that we'd try to find something and bring it back."

Adnan picked up the story. "That was a week ago, so I'm pretty sure they have given up on us by now. It's really hard in the city. At first, the Red Cross had stations set up for people to go to, but pretty soon they ran out of food too. And nobody wanted to volunteer because they needed to look after themselves. All the stores have been broken into and looted, there's nothing left on the shelves, so if you weren't the first ones there you got nothing. Some people are selling cans of food and things like candles, but you need money or something of value to trade, and our families don't have either."

Tony asked kindly, "How many people in your families did you leave?

"I have my mom and little sister…she's five" Tom answered. He ran a hand through his shaggy hair. "Adnan's mom has four little ones and his dad is sick so he can't get up."

"Sick how?"

Adnan stared at the tiled floor. "He fell at work and broke his leg. Plus, I think he's depressed. If there is no work, there's no paycheck and he hates my mom having to go to work."

"How old are you?" Monica asked.

"We're both fifteen."

"In grade ten?"

"Yep." Adnan and Tom both nodded. "When there was a school to go to."

Jason reached over and patted both boys on their shoulders. "You did the right thing by going to look for food. But you've probably figured out we're too far away to help them now."

"We could give you something to take back," Irma said doubtfully. "But it took you a week to get here, so it's a week back. Anything we gave you would be all gone by the time you got there."

"Yep." Tony nodded. "You forget how far a hundred miles is when all you have to do is jump in the car. You boys will have to stay here until this power thing is straightened out." He looked at his wife. "Where can we put them, Mother?"

"First we put them in a tub." She wrinkled her nose. "Then I suggest they sleep in the attic. Monica and Jason need his old room, and the other bedroom only has a single bed. They can make beds with some extra blankets. And it'll be warm up there next to the chimney."

The boys hung their heads. Tom said, "Thanks, but we should go home. Our moms will be so worried."

"You can go if you want," Jason answered. "But you know how hard it was getting here. Things won't be changed there."

"You stay here with us," Irma said kindly. "Maybe this'll all be over soon. Your moms would want you to be safe."

She looked at Tony. "Why don't you light a fire in the fire pit? I hate to waste propane heating water and there are five people here in desperate need of a bath. Jason, come and fill that old tub, we can heat the water in that and then you can either dunk yourselves in that or carry the water up to the bathroom. Your choice." She eyed the two boys. "I think we can find you some shirts and underclothes that fit. You can wash your jeans later."

Tony gave the boys a wink. "Better listen to Mother," he said. "She's the boss around here.

When the newcomers had all had a much-needed bath, and beds had been arranged, the family met in the kitchen for supper. Baby Jack held court from his father's old high chair at the head of the table. Happily, he banged his spoon on the tray while his parents and grandparents smiled indulgently.

"This is delicious. Thank you, Mrs. Baldini." Tom politely folded his napkin and placed it beside his plate. "It's been a long time since I had meat."

"Me too." Jason patted his stomach. "You outdid yourself, Mom."

"I'm glad you enjoyed it." Irma passed around the teapot. "Now that you are all clean and fed, I'd like to hear how things are out in the world."

"It's a nightmare," Monica spoke first. "You are so lucky to be out here. For the first couple of weeks, people went along, almost as normal, waiting for everything to get back to the way it was. Then as time went on, the stores were empty, the food depots closed, there's no transportation, no communication. People are getting desperate and we could see it was time to get away from there."

Jason nodded and grimaced. "The trip out here was a real eye-opener too. When everything quit, bam, there were thousands of people on the roads and highways. We stuck to country roads as much as possible, but even there, there are abandoned vehicles all over. At least on the back roads, people drive slower, so most of them were okay, just stranded."

"Did you talk to anybody?" his Dad asked.

They both nodded. "A few people came out to talk to us, looking for news. And at night if we saw a farmhouse we asked if we could stay there." Jason looked at his baby son. "It's still warm out, but we wanted to get Jack inside if we could. We shared some of our food the first few times, but then it was all gone, so we just walked until we got here. The last two nights we slept outside."

"What about you two?" Irma asked the teens. "Were you able to find shelter?"

They shook their heads. "We raided a couple of gardens," Tom admitted sheepishly. "And once we asked someone for food. But mostly we just followed Jason and Monica and stayed out of sight."

"Not very well." Jason laughed. "I spotted them on the second day and I knew they were behind us." He glared at the boys. "It's a good thing you didn't try to steal from us. You might have been hurt."

"We saw where you left the wagon," Adnan said. "But there was nothing in it except some blankets and pictures."

"It just got too hard to pull." Monica looked sad. "I wanted to bring the pictures, but at the end, it all comes down to what helps you survive. But I don't know why you didn't keep the blankets. Sleeping on the ground they would have come in handy."

"How are people coping on the farms?" asked Tony.

"About the same as you." Jason reached over and lifted Jack from his chair. "Most farmers have the wherewithal to live through tough times. After all, we managed without electricity or motorized vehicles for thousands of years. It's the city folk who fall apart."

Irma stood up and began to clear away the used plates. "Enough doom and gloom for today." She announced. "I know you are all exhausted so it's off to bed with you. We'll have lots of time to visit."

"And boys," she stopped with a handful of dishes. "Don't forget to say your prayers and thank God for your good fortune in finding us."

They both ducked their heads as they moved towards the stairs. "We will, Mrs. Baldini. Good night and thank you."

CHAPTER SEVEN

From the window, the softly falling snow was beautiful. Fluffy white flakes floated slowly to the ground, sticking to every tree branch and fence post. Later, when the moon rose, the whole yard would be transformed into a sparkling fairyland.

Monica shivered involuntarily, as she watched the world turn white. The thermometer hanging outside registered minus ten Celsius. Winter was truly here. She glanced down, checking that Jack was not too close to the heater.

She was so thankful that her father-in-law was such a packrat. Searches of the shed and the old barn had unearthed a treasure trove of useful items. One of them was an old steel barrel that with the help of some stove pipe and a metal saw, had been turned into a wood-burning stove.

Tony had flattened the top of the barrel so they could put a kettle or pot on top of it. A door had been fashioned from an old piece of steel that he had found. The flue consisted of a circle cut out of a water pail, welded to a steel rod, and inserted into the stovepipe. Connected to the old brick chimney, it kept the living room and the upstairs toasty warm. All they had to do was keep the fire burning all day and all night.

Sighing, Monica opened the steel door and added another log. She poured hot water into her cup. They had used the last tea bag, a week ago, so now it was plain hot water to drink. She took a sip, thankful for even this small comfort. She couldn't imagine what would have happened to them if they hadn't left the city.

She saw Tony and Adnan approaching the back door each carrying an armful of split wood. Their breath formed tiny crystals in the air. Quickly, she made her way to the door and opened it just wide enough for them to enter.

"Cold enough to freeze a witch's tit, hey Adnan?" laughed Tony, as he made his way to the wood box in the corner of the living room.

The boy nodded and agreed. They both removed their snow-covered boots and set them on the mat in front of the door.

Monica sighed and began to mop up the trail of water they had created.

Taking off his heavy coat Tony commented. "The boy is getting pretty good with an axe, for someone who had never seen one before."

"I'd seen one." Adnan protested. "On my games pad and on TV."

They all laughed. Tom and Adnan had both worn blisters on both hands while they learned to wield an axe. "Where is everybody?" the boy asked as he dropped to the floor beside the baby.

Monica waved her arm vaguely. "Mom is upstairs having a nap before supper. Tom and Jason decided to walk over to the Johnson's and check on them. They figured that it was warm enough, but I don't think they counted on the snow."

She turned away, trying to hide her troubled face. "They've been gone a long time."

"It's early yet," Tony comforted. "It gets dark so early these days we forget it's only four o'clock. They left at two, and it takes a good hour to walk, so they'll be along by supper time."

"Which will be in an hour?" Irma said as she came down the stairs "I didn't mean to sleep so long. Tony, can you light the lamp in the kitchen?"

"Of course,", he left the warmth of the living room and followed her into the kitchen. While it wasn't fully dark yet, the sun had been obscured by the heavy snow and the kitchen was shadowy and cold. He walked with sure steps to the table where another of his "treasures" rested.

"The oil for this lamp is nearly all gone," he observed. "We'll need to go back to candles pretty soon."

"Yes, I know." His wife pulled a paper bag of potatoes towards her. "The propane isn't going to hold out much longer either, and it's only December. There could be a lot of cold days between now and spring."

He came up behind her, set the lamp closer to the sink, and put both hands on her shoulders.

"Don't worry, Mother." He soothed. "I'm sure the government or somebody is working to get us back up and running. We'll have heat and lights soon."

She laughed. "Tell that to Jack. He might believe you."

"Do you think the boys are okay?" she continued, worry evident in her voice. "It shouldn't take that long to check on Sam and Stella."

She placed the last potato in the pot, covered them with water and reached for the matches to light the range.

Her husband patted her shoulder one more time and moved towards the back door. "I'll just check the driveway," he said. "Maybe they're having trouble in the snow."

She laughed softly. "They won't have trouble in the snow," she chuckled. "But you can certainly take another look up the road for them."

The old couple both jumped, as the back door swung open with a crash. They rushed towards the group standing in the doorway. Monica came flying from the living room, concern etched on her face. In the doorway, Jason supported Stella Johnson as he set down a large suitcase. Behind him, Tom and Sam Johnson had their arms full of boxes and bags.

Irma put her arms around her friend, noticing how thin she was. "Come in, come in." She dropped her arms and took a cold hand in her own. "You're just in time for supper." She glanced up at her son, who gave a tired smile.

"Sam and Stella can't stay over on the farm." He said as he gently removed the older woman's heavy coat.

"They can't heat that barn and the cows aren't producing milk anyway. So, we opened the door and all the gates so they can try to forage and get through the winter on their own." He wiped his forehead which glistened with sweat, despite the cold.

"They have to stay with us until things straighten out. Do we have a bed they can have?"

"Of course we have a bed." His mother bristled a bit at the thought that he would doubt it for a moment. "Monica, finish the vegetables, will you? Just add enough for two more. And, Tony run up and open the back bedroom. I think the bed is made up, but there are extra blankets in the hall closet."

"It's only a single bed," she apologized to Stella. "But you'll keep warmer that way."

Taking her arm, she led the way into the living room where the fire crackled in the woodstove. Neither of them had said anything, seeming content to let others tell them what to do for now. They both moved closer to the fire, holding out their hands and keeping their eyes on the worn carpet.

Tom and Jason removed their own coats and boots and began to carry the bundles and suitcase up the narrow staircase. Monica busied herself at the stove, poking at the potatoes to see if they were soft. Tony returned from his errand upstairs and began to set the table, adding two place settings to the six that had been there. He couldn't see into the living room but could hear the soft murmur of his wife's voice as she comforted their guests.

He was worried. Another two mouths to feed would seriously deplete their supplies. The vegetables in the root cellar were still plentiful and they had the meat his wife had worked so hard canning. But it was only December and, in this country, winter could last a long time. He couldn't remember when it had been so cold or snowed so heavily this early in the year.

Of course, they couldn't turn their neighbours away. Any more than they could have refused shelter to Tom and Adnan when they had shown up, tired and dirty on the doorstep.

Behind him, Monica was opening a jar of peas and humming to herself. The smell of onions and the sizzle of the frying pan filled the kitchen. Tony sniffed appreciatively.

"I'm sure glad Jason had the idea to dig out the old root cellar," he observed. "If we had left our food in the garage, it would be frozen solid by now."

"Yes." Monica poured the peas into a pot. "The crawl space under the house didn't look very safe, but those old pioneers knew about storing stuff through winters. All the root cellar needed was some shoring up and a little more digging. Tom and Adnan did their fair share too."

He chuckled. "Those hands hadn't held more than a TV remote or a phone, but they soon learned how to work."

"It's a good thing everybody made it home." He added. "It's snowing harder than ever. I can barely see the path to the root cellar and barn."

Monica joined him looking out the kitchen window. "You're right, Dad. If I didn't know it was there, I would never find the root cellar door." She turned away and began to remove pots from the stove. "We'll have to make sure that path stays clear. It won't do any good to have food stored if we can't get to it."

She raised her voice slightly. "Dinner's ready. Come and get it."

"Come on." Irma bustled into the kitchen holding Stella's arm lightly. "Sit down and eat and then we'll have a nice cup of hot water and talk."

Stella looked up. "I brought tea." I'll just run up and get it. There are the last of our tea bags and about a pound of coffee in the grocery bag."

"Coffee!!" Jason grinned. "I'll go get it. I've been missing coffee the most."

"No rush. Eat first and then we'll have tea for a treat." Irma pointed to the chairs at the end of the table. "You sit there, Stella. Sam, you sit beside her. The rest of us will shift over. Jack's high chair will fit at the corner. Father, will you say Grace?"

Tony looked at her in surprise. "We're saying Grace?"

She nodded. "I think we need all the help we can get. A prayer now and then won't hurt."

Everybody bowed their heads as Tony recited a simple prayer of thanks.

Picking up their forks, they again discussed the situation.

"What do you suppose has happened?" asked Irma, poking at her potato. "Sam have you heard anything new?"

Sam shook his head. "Nope. I've probably heard the same rumours as you. Without real news, it's hard to say. But I remember reading something a few months ago about EMP attacks being possible."

"What's that?" asked Adnan.

"EMP is an electromagnetic pulse." Monica was forever the teacher. "Presumably it's when a warhead goes off in the air, sending out high energy waves that fry any electronics they pass through. The North American grid could be wiped out in an instant."

"Who would do that?" Adnan was interested.

"Probably somebody who doesn't like the USA," Monica answered. "And of course, Canada is in the same grid so we share the pain."

"But," she continued, "it doesn't even have to be another country. It could come from a solar flare or even an accidental event from some military installation."

Sam grunted as he speared a piece of potato. "Probably those A-rabs. They hate us bad enough." He glanced at Adnan. "Brown people...can't trust 'em."

The others glanced at each other, but Adnan kept his eyes on his plate, seeming oblivious to Sam's comment.

Tony stopped chewing and interjected. "You know I remember watching a TV show about something called HAARP. It's supposed to analyze the heat of the ionosphere by transmitting radio beams into the sky. There are theories that this could disrupt the electric power around the world."

Jason spoke up from where he was feeding the baby at the end of the table. "I remember seeing that show. It seemed farfetched to me. Why would the government try to ruin their own country?"

His father answered sarcastically. "It seemed farfetched, but here we are freezing in the dark and wondering how to survive the winter so maybe those crackpot conspiracy theorists were on to something."

"We're pretty lucky," Monica added. "I'd hate to be outside in the cold right now. Here we are warm and cozy and we have enough to get us through the next couple of months." She got up and closed the curtains.

Irma sighed then stood up and began to clear the plates from the table.

"Enough of that, "she said. "Let's clear the table and play a game." She spoke over her shoulder as she carried a stack of dishes over to the sink. "Come on, we can do the dishes in the morning. What game shall we play? Or we can just tell stories until bed, but no more conspiracy theories or farfetched ideas. I'm sick of this whole discussion."

Sam pushed back his chair and spoke to his wife. "Don't just sit there like a lump. Go get that tea."

Irma frowned when Stella leaped to her feet and rushed upstairs.

"I'll put Jack to bed." Jason picked up the baby and wiped his face. "Come on, Buddy."

When he reappeared a few minutes later he was carrying his old guitar.

"Look what I found." He held it up gleefully. "I haven't seen this for years."

"It's always been in the corner of your room," Irma answered. "Do you think you can still play?"

"Of course, it's like riding a bike." He began to strum a tune. "I wonder if there are any strings around?"

Soon they were all sipping weak tea and being serenaded as Jason tried to remember his old music lessons. Sam dealt cards around the table in preparation for a game of crib.

Tony looked around the dark kitchen. "You know," he commented. "We should move the table into the living room. It's warmer in there and then we only need one lamp."

"Good idea." Jason nodded. "We could push the couch back and move the bookshelf in here. And, Dad, aren't there more leaves for this table? If we move it into the other room there would be room to stretch it out."

"We'll do that tomorrow." Tony nodded. "It should only take a few minutes if we all pitch in."

CHAPTER EIGHT

In the morning, snow still fell, coating the shed and the now useless cars with a new beauty. A strip of blue sky showed in the west, giving the whole scene a bluish tinge and promising a sunny afternoon. The mountains, which had been a dark green only a week before, were now covered with a white blanket.

Tony ripped the blue tarpaulin off the woodpile in preparation to adding another layer of split logs.

All the men were bundled up in their warmest coats and sturdiest boots, ready to do a little logging. Jason and the boys carried axes over their shoulders. Sam carried an old cross-cut saw which had been unearthed in the shed.

"Sorry, Sam. It's the old fashioned way now." Tony shrugged. "the electric pull doesn't work on the chain saw, just like the cars that don't start."

"It's okay," Sam answered. "It'll do us good to get some exercise. I should have brought that old chain saw from my barn. It starts with an old fashioned magneto."

As the group turned to make their way to the nearby trees, they were startled by the sound of voices behind them. "Helloooo!" someone called.

Tony turned to confront the newcomer. "Hello. What can we do for you?"

The man who had spoken held out his hand to shake. Behind him stood five young, bearded men, dressed in ill-fitting winter clothing.

Jason moved forward to stand beside his father.

"We've been working our way out here," The man gave Tony a hearty handshake. "We had bikes, but in this snow, it's impossible to ride them, so it's foot power now. I'm Nick," he added.

The two groups eyed each other warily. Jason stepped forward, letting the axe drop into his hand. "Have you heard any news?" he asked.

"No." Nick shook his head. "the city is in chaos with everybody out for themselves. There's no food or heat and people are melting snow for water." He waved his hand, indicating the group behind him. "We're all friends, so we decided to hit the road. Say, have you got any food? We haven't eaten for a while."

Jason silently appraised the men. They didn't look like "friends". They looked like a gang of hoodlums to him. He would lay bets that they were carrying some kind of weapons under their heavy coats. He shifted the axe in his hand and hoped the boys had done the same.

Sam stepped forward to join his hosts "You guys look hungry." He held out his own calloused hand. "We're pretty stretched here," he said. "But there's an empty farmhouse about a mile away. It's mine, and I'd be happy for someone to stay in it for a while. There's cattle there and chickens that need feeding".

And" he added, "I'm pretty sure there's still some vegetables in the pantry. They probably froze, but that won't matter. Just light a fire in the fireplace and cook 'em up."

"How come you left it?" Nick asked suspiciously.

"I'm old." Sam shrugged. "Me and my wife couldn't cope alone so we came to join our friends. If nobody is there, I have to go back every day and check on the animals. You'd be doing me a favour."

"We're not farmers." One of the strangers spoke up. "We need food in cans, not on the hoof."

"There are no cans left," Jason answered. "What wasn't eaten, exploded in the cold. Sam's right, we don't have anything here to share, but over at his farm, you can help yourself to whatever there is."

The men glanced at each other, then at Nick, who seemed to be their leader. He shrugged and nodded. "Okay, we'll try that." He spoke to the

54

bearded man at his shoulder. "Didn't you learn how to butcher a cow, Trevor?"

"Well, I butchered a deer when me and my dad went hunting." Trevor nodded. "It's probably the same."

"I'll draw you a map." Sam took a stick and began to draw in the snow. "It's not far. Follow the road east, then turn at the second intersection. The mailbox has my name on it, Johnson. The key is hanging in the barn, behind the door."

When the strangers had left, the three men and two teenagers relaxed, their shoulders sagging in relief.

"That's not good," Jason observed watching as they reached the end of the driveway. "Those guys looked as if they would take what they wanted and to hell with the rest of us."

"I agree." His dad said and Sam nodded. "Thanks for handing over your house, Sam. You know they will probably destroy it."

"I don't care about that," Sam said. "I just wanted them away from here. And of course, I still have to go over and check on my cows. Those hooligans probably won't even know which end to feed."

Tony looked at the house and saw three anxious women peering through the window. "I'm putting my shotgun by the front door." He said quietly. "And I think one of us should stay around the house all the time."

The others nodded.

"You young guys continue on and get us some wood." Tony continued. "Sam and I will go tell the women what's going on and maybe check over our resources."

"I think we'll cut wood at the end of the driveway today." Jason nodded to the two boys. "I'd like to know where those guys went."

CHAPTER NINE

After the evening meal had been cleared, the family remained gathered around the table. The men had moved it from the kitchen, and now they had more room to stretch out. A single lamp cast a dim light, leaving the corners of the room in total darkness.

"This is better." Tony looked around approvingly. "Warm and cozy."

The others nodded.

"We've been pretty lucky so far," he said. "But I'd still like to know how or why this happened".

"I'm going with the aliens," Adnan spoke up. "What else could make the whole world stop working?"

"Well, there are a number of things, actually". Monica smiled across at him. "There are accidents to the power grid, solar flares, disruptions to the ionosphere. Even bombs from another country could have disrupted the whole world."

"And remember," Jason held up a cautionary hand, "we don't know it's the whole world. Maybe it's only around here, or the country, or North America." He sighed deeply. "I just wish we knew more."

Everybody was silent. They had gone over this so many times, together and separately.

"We need to go and find out what's happening." Jason clasped his wife's hand. "One or two of us should walk to the nearest police station. Surely, they will have learned something there. I could go tomorrow."

Irma shook her head. "No. It can't be you, Jason. You have a baby son to think of. There's two feet of snow on the ground and you know the weather can change in an instant. I couldn't bear to think of you lost or in danger."

"I'll go."

All eyes turned to the neighbour who had joined them so recently.

Sam nodded resolutely. "I'll go. You are all at home here, but I'm just visiting. I need to know if I'll have a life to go back to, or if we should just pack it in."

"Well one thing we know," Tony grinned wryly. "Your house will probably be a complete loss after those motorcyclists are in it for a while. You might have saved our lives by offering it to them. Who knows what their intentions were? So," he continued "Don't say you are just a visitor. You are part of this group…. this family."

Then he turned to his son. "And don't think you can just walk anywhere, Jason. It's ten miles each way, through snowbanks and whatever else is waiting out there. We saw one gang. Maybe there are more holed up somewhere waiting for warmer weather. We can't risk you, son."

Jason nodded thoughtfully, as he acknowledged his parents' comments.

"I'm going," Sam said. "I can walk over to my place and saddle one of the horses. If I go early in the morning, I'll be able to sneak by those guys. I can check on the cows at the same time. Those city slickers are probably keeping pretty close to the house. On horseback, I should be there and back in a few hours."

"You can't go alone," Adnan spoke up. "Tom or I will go with you."

The others nodded.

"Good idea," Jason agreed. "Have either of you ever ridden a horse?"

Heads dropped.

"No."

"Doesn't matter. All you have to do is hang on to me." Sam had apparently agreed to the plan.

"If the weather is okay, we'll leave in the morning. Which one of you is coming with me?"

The two boys glanced at each other. Both were eager to leave the farmhouse for an excursion. With eight adults and one baby, plus a dog that masqueraded as a rug, they were starting to feel a bit claustrophobic.

"Can we both go?" Tom asked.

"No." Sam was firm. "The horse can only carry two of us, and even that's not ideal for a long distance."

"How about drawing cards?" asked Irma. "High card goes, low card stays here and chops wood."

She reached for the deck of cards which were conveniently kept on the coffee table, next to the crib board. Expertly she began to shuffle the deck while the boys moved closer.

When she had finished shuffling, she fanned the cards and held them out. "Okay, draw, but don't show your card until you both have one."

Nervously Tom and Adnan reached out and drew two cards from the deck. They flipped them over at the same moment and Tom whooped with glee.

"Ten! I get to go!"

Gloomily Adnan looked at his two of clubs.

"Well," Monica consoled the disappointed boy. "Just think of him eating a cold sandwich, while you have a hot meal in a nice warm house."

Only Stella noticed the sigh of relief from her husband. For a moment their eyes met, and then she lowered her head submissively.

The next day dawned bright and clear. Once again, the thermometer hanging outside the kitchen window registered minus 10C.

The two envoys were up and out by the time the rest of the family made their way to the living room. The fire crackled merrily and the smell of coffee permeated the house.

As she poured the coffee, Irma said, "Enjoy this. It's the last of the coffee and I've already used the grounds three times."

Tony took a sip and grimaced. "Not much taste left." He sipped the hot drink again. "But at least it's hot and the smell makes you think it's a normal day."

"What's normal anymore?" Irma sat beside him at the table. Then changing the subject; "I hope Sam and Tom are okay. I gave them some jam sandwiches to take with them. And that's the last of the bread."

"Did you send a thermos?"

"Of course. It has the same watery brew we're enjoying, in it. I'm sure after a couple of hours on a horse, it'll taste much better."

They were soon all gathered around the table, the baby in his customary place between his parents.

Monica spooned cereal into his waiting mouth while the adults all watched fondly. Adnan yawned widely and reached for a piece of bread, then hesitated as he noticed nobody else was eating.

"Go ahead, Dear." Irma pushed the plate closer to him. "You're a growing boy, and you have a strenuous day ahead of you."

He didn't wait to be asked twice and began to slather the homemade raspberry jam on a large slice.

"Are we going to chop wood?" he asked.

"Don't talk with food in your mouth," Monica spoke automatically, then grinned sheepishly. "Sorry, I can't help being a mom."

"It's okay…you're right." He smiled back.

"And yes, we are going to cut wood. It's a never-ending job if we want to keep warm." She turned to her mother-in-law. "Do you mind watching the baby, Mom? I need to get some exercise or I'm going to go crazy."

"Of course." She looked at Stella who hadn't said a word so far this morning. "We'll be able to handle one small baby, won't we, Stella?"

A tear slipped from the other woman's faded eyes, but she didn't answer.

"They'll be fine!" Tony reached across the table and patted her hand. "You'll see; they'll be back before we know it with some kind of news."

"You don't know that", she whispered. "Who knows what those hooligans over at our house will do if they catch them?" She stood up. "And it's so cold. Why didn't the young guys go instead of sending poor S..s..Sam out in the freezing cold?"

"I'm going back to bed," she continued. "It's warm there and I need to be alone."

The rest of them looked after her with dismay.

"Don't go to bed," Irma called softly. "I think we are nearly out of propane and I want to cook up the rest of the vegetables before the stove quits. You can help me."

"No, no, you look after your family." She disappeared up the narrow staircase.

"She'll be okay." Jason spoke up, "It had to be Sam to go. He knows his horses and plus he volunteered."

"And now", he stood up decisively. "Let's go and get some wood before this fire goes out. From what Mom says, we may be cooking on it before too long."

Tony stood too and called to the old dog who was dozing under the heater. "C'mon Rufus, you need some exercise too."

When Irma had been left alone, she carried little Jack into the kitchen and put him in the old playpen she had liberated from the attic. The bottom was thickly lined with blankets to protect it from the unheated floor.

Glumly she opened the pantry and began to remove the carrots and potatoes from their bins. She hoped there was enough propane left to cook them. There were more in the root cellar that Jason had dug in the fall, but unless things changed, they might be eating them raw. She surveyed the few cans left on the shelves.

"Best eat them up before they freeze," she thought to herself and placed them on the counter too. There was a bit of meat still frozen in the garage, so she could cook it all and have a stew. Then the whole pot could go into the garage where it would freeze solid.

Her spirits began to lift and she hummed a little tune. Behind her, Jack laughed at his own private joke, and she smiled.

"It's not so bad," she thought. "We'll have a nice stew. No more flour so no bread anymore, but I think there's some rice left. And there's cereal for the baby. No milk, of course, but we can survive a while longer"

With her arms full, she turned and let out a scream as she nearly bumped into a stranger. The cans dropped from her hands and rolled across the old linoleum.

"Don't scream, Lady." One of his large hands pointed a pistol at her. Her eyes darted towards the baby who was watching in fascination.

"Okay. What do you want?"

"Food. And I see you have lots of it here."

"No, no, I don't." she watched his lips move in the tangled beard. His eyes were steady and focussed on her. "there really isn't much food left," she continued her voice shaking. "We have six men to feed and this is the last of it."

"Well, now you only have one man to feed….me!" He waved the gun in her direction. "I watched everybody leave so I know you're alone here."

He glanced towards the playpen. "I don't want to hurt anybody, but I haven't eaten for a few days and here you are all warm and fed. It's not fair!"

"I'll be happy to feed you," Irma made her voice soft and she hoped, soothing. "Just put the gun away. You don't need to threaten me. There's some coffee left in the pot and I can give you some canned fruit while the vegetables cook."

"Just..." her voice rose…" put the gun away. You're scaring the baby."

"I'm not interested in fruit and coffee", he growled. "I'm taking it all. I don't know what's happening in the world right now, but I want to be prepared for the worst."

Out of the corner of her eye, Irma saw movement in the dark stairwell behind the intruder. Stella must have heard the crash when the cans fell on the floor.

She moved a little closer to the baby and the man turned his head. Good, he wasn't looking towards the stairs at all. The gun became her sole focus and she kept her eyes riveted on it. She didn't see the guitar until it crashed down on the intruder's head.

He fell heavily to the floor and the gun dropped from his hand.

Stella moved into the room and gave it a kick so it spun across the linoleum and lodged against the playpen.

"Oh my God!" Irma grabbed the gun and with shaking hands aimed it in the direction of the bearded man.

"Quick let's tie him up with something." Stella's urgent voice seemed to come from far away. "He might wake up in a minute."

The two elderly women looked around desperately. What did they have to tie up an angry and very big man?

"Toaster cord." Irma grabbed the toaster and quickly cut off the cord with the knife that she used for chopping vegetables. They grabbed the man's arms and pulled them together behind his back.

"What about his feet?"

"Quick, get the cord off the kettle." Irma handed the knife to her friend.

When he was safely trussed up, the two women grinned at each other. "Stella, you were like the avenging angel there", Irma said. "But I don't think Jason is going to be playing that guitar any time soon."

"Yes, it's a good thing he left it beside the stairs." Stella sat on a kitchen chair and wiped her forehead with a shaky hand. "I couldn't believe it when I came down and saw you being held at gunpoint. All I could think of was some movie I saw where the heroine saved the day by knocking some guy out with a poker. But the guitar was all I could reach."

"Well, it worked."

At their feet, the man groaned.

A trickle of blood from his forehead was staining the floor. Irma moved back in case he could escape. They weren't the most expert of knot tiers and she had no idea if the cords would hold him if he struggled hard enough.

Now that he was helpless, he didn't look quite so fearsome. It was the beard, she decided, but all the men had beards. It was too hard to shave in cold water and besides, they said it helped keep their faces warm. She also noted how thin he was under his bulky clothing.

She still held the pistol in her lap and absently she thumbed the magazine. It dropped open and to her surprise, there were no bullets in it.

Irma's fear began to be replaced by pity. His groans had subsided so she gave him a nudge with her foot and said "what were you thinking coming in here and threatening an old lady and a baby with a gun?"

Stella smiled. Irma thought she sounded fierce, but nobody would mistake the softness in her voice for anything other than motherly concern.

He groaned again. "I'm sorry, lady. What did you hit me with anyway?"

"I didn't hit you. My friend hit you with a guitar. Another old lady I might add and my son is going to be really upset over his guitar. He's had it since he was eight years old."

"I'm sorry," he groaned again. "Can I get up now?"

"No!" the women spoke simultaneously

"Not until you answer my question. Why were you here threatening us?"

"You don't know how it is out there." He answered. "I left my wife and son yesterday. They just couldn't walk anymore. There's no food left in the city, and no heat in our apartment. Everybody is just running wild, trying to survive."

He took a deep breath. "I just wanted some food to take back to them."

"Well, why didn't you just ask?" Irma asked indignantly. "We don't have much, but we wouldn't leave anyone to starve."

She bent over. "Okay, I'll let you up, and we'll fix that cut on your head."

"No bullets in here." She laid the pistol on the table. "but I do have a loaded shotgun." She nodded towards the corner and Stella, taking her cue, grabbed the shotgun and pointed it at the intruder.

"Are you sure?" Stella asked "He could still try to hurt us and steal everything."

"Let him try." Irma began loosening the cords around his wrists.

"He's not going to hurt us, is he?" and she glared at her prisoner.

He stood up and sheepishly shook his head. Under the bushy beard and unkempt hair, his lips curled in a smile and blue eyes twinkled. "Brought down by a couple of grannies and a baby!" He shook his head again. "No, you're safe from me."

"Okay. Our water still runs even if it's cold, so go and wash that cut off at the sink. I'll find some peroxide to clean it with and get you something to eat. Then we'll see what we can do about your family."

CHAPTER TEN

When the wood cutters returned, they were surprised to find a bushy haired man sitting at the kitchen counter slurping soup. Irma bustled around the room, slicing vegetables and putting them into a large, simmering pot. Stella held Jack on her lap, spooning mashed carrots into his mouth, and smiling at the man.

Jason glared at him suspiciously as he removed his coat and hung it on the hook. "Who's he?"

The others crowded in behind him.

"Is that our last can of soup?" demanded Monica. "The one we were saving for Jack?"

"Yes," Irma answered her. "And we need to get some more carrots from the root cellar too".

"Oh, come in and sit down." The others were still clustered in the doorway, watching their new guest.

"This is George, and he needs help." She decided to keep the story of how he had asked, for later.

Tony rubbed his hands and came over to hug his wife. "Well, we never turned anyone away who needed help, did we?"

"What's your story, young man?"

George nervously pushed the empty bowl away. "Thank you, ma'am." He said. He turned towards the older man.

"It's my wife," he said. "I left her in an abandoned house about two hours walk from here. We left our apartment in the city to look for food, but she got so tired she just couldn't continue. Your wife," and he nodded towards Irma, "was kind enough to give me some soup, but I have to go back to Melanie and my son right away."

"We'll have some lunch and then we'll go get her," Jason assured him. "Can she walk do you think or will we need to carry her?"

"Go in the living room," Irma waved her hands dismissively. "I can't think with all of you in here. Plus, the fire needs building up. Sorry, the last of the coffee went this morning, but I think there should be hot water on top of the heater to warm yourselves up."

When the room had cleared of everybody except herself and Stella, she muttered, "I don't know what to give them for lunch. The bread is all gone and I can't bake more without propane. The stew isn't done yet, and they need something hot."

"They'll have to settle for hot water to drink." Stella came over and put her arm around her friend. "I'm sorry I was such a bitch this morning. I'm just so worried about Sam and that boy. Do you think they are okay?"

"They'll be fine". Irma patted her hand. "I wonder if I should try making pancakes with the last of the flour?"

"I don't think so. What if the stove quits before you finish cooking them? Then you will have used all the flour for nothing." Stella opened the pantry door as if hoping that something had magically appeared on the empty shelves.

"My mom used to say, anyone can cook with food," Stella continued. "It's a real art to feed people without it."

Irma laughed.

"Well, your mom was right. Do you see anything in there?"

"An old can of cocoa. Do we have any sugar left?"

"Maybe half a cup. Okay, cocoa to drink, that'll help a bit. Then they will have to wait for the vegetables to cook. We need to send something to George's wife and son too, so they have enough strength to get back here."

Just then the flame on the old range gave one last flare and went out. The two women looked at each other with dismay.

"Well, that just doubled the time it will take to cook anything." Irma huffed. "I hated cooking on a wood stove when I was young, and I don't suppose it has improved with time."

"Let's just spoon the stew into a smaller pot," Stella suggested. "We'll just cook enough for now and the rest can sit on the heater and simmer."

Soon they were sitting at the table with the rest of the family, all nursing cups of watery cocoa. The stew simmered on the wood stove, filling the room with delicious smells that only added to their hunger.

George said apologetically, "I'm sorry I ate your last can of soup. I didn't know."

"Of course you didn't," Irma patted his hand. "How could you? Don't worry we'll be okay. Now, what did you decide about George's wife?" She addressed the table at large.

"Adnan and I are going with George to get her and bring her back here," Jason answered. "Hopefully she can walk, but with three of us, we'll be able to carry her if necessary"

"We'll send a thermos of hot cocoa and some stew with you." Stella piped up.

"You'll need to go soon," Tony said. "It's already mid-afternoon and the sun goes down at four."

"Maybe you should wait until morning?" Monica added her voice. "Sam and Tom should be back tonight with the horse and you can ride over. That'll be quicker in the long run."

They all looked at George.

"I hate to leave her alone another night." He spoke slowly "Why don't I go alone and bring them back tomorrow?"

"And what if she's can't walk another ten miles?" Jason stood up. "No, I think we should all go. I know if it was my wife and son, I'd be sick until I knew they were okay. We can camp overnight and come back in the morning if we have to."

"Is that stew ready, Mom?" he asked. "I'm anxious to get on the way now."

"It might be a bit underdone" his mother answered. "But let's try a bit."

When the men had left for their long walk through the snow, the old people sat and looked at each other across the table. Monica had gone upstairs to change and left the baby sleeping in his playpen.

"I don't know if that was a good idea," Tony said slowly. "We didn't really know if that guy was telling the truth."

The women glanced at each other.

"Okay, what's up?" asked Tony "You both look like you have a secret."

Just then Monica came into the room carrying the broken guitar. "What happened to Jason's guitar?" She held it up and poked her hand through a hole in the frame.

"Well…" Stella began.

"There is a bit of a story behind that", Irma continued.

After hearing the story of how George came to be in the house, Tony looked troubled.

"I wish you had told us that before Jason and Adnan went off with him." He said. "How do we know there are a wife and son, and not a plot to separate us?"

"Oh, I'm sure he's telling the truth." Irma tried to convince him. Now she was beginning to have her own doubts. "The gun wasn't even loaded."

"Gun?" Monica leaped to her feet. "He had a gun?"

"He doesn't have it now." Stella went and retrieved the handgun from where they had hidden it in the china cabinet. "See, it's still here and it's not loaded."

"That doesn't mean he doesn't have another one." Monica began to pull on her boots. "I'm going after them. Jason needs to know about this so he can be alert."

"They've been gone for almost an hour." Irma protested.

"I don't care. They will have left a trail in the snow and if I hurry I can catch up to them." She fumbled in her pockets. "Do we have another flashlight? I gave mine to Jason."

Silently Irma handed her the one she kept in the kitchen.

Just before she wrapped her scarf around her face, Monica tried to reassure them. "I'll only go for an hour. If I don't catch up to them by then, I'll come back. In the meantime, you lock the doors and don't let any more vagabonds in."

She hated to leave them. Three elderly people and one baby weren't much defence if someone really wanted in. However, and involuntarily she smiled, those two old ladies had done quite a number on George. "And the guitar", she almost laughed out loud as she left the driveway.

Thankfully, the men had left a clear trail for her and she could move much faster than they would have, breaking a new trail through the snow and carrying supplies. She hurried forward.

From the window, Irma, Stella and Tony watched until she was out of sight. It was three o'clock and already the light was fading.

"I'm going to bring in some more wood." Tony turned away from the window.

Irma put her arm around Stella's thin shoulders. "You did good." She told her. "You're stronger than you think."

"Am I?" Stella hugged her back. "I've heard for years how stupid and weak I am. I don't even know how I managed to hit a man."

"You are not stupid, and definitely not weak. I was standing there like an idiot and you just barrelled in and saved the day. Now let's go get some blankets and figure out where George and his family are going to sleep."

It was full dark when Monica returned. Jack was in his pyjamas and sleeping soundly after a supper of mashed vegetables.

"Did you catch them?" Irma asked anxiously as she helped her daughter-in-law remove her coat and scarf.

"No," Monica shook her head. "I thought I heard voices at one point, but I never saw anybody. It was getting dark, so I turned around." She gave Irma a quick hug. "I'm sure they are okay, Mom. I thought about it while I was walking and if anything was going to happen, it would probably be close to here. There would be no sense in walking that far if he only wanted to steal something."

"Do you have any of that stew left? I'm starving."

"Of course." Irma bustled into the kitchen to get a bowl, then spooned a generous helping from the pot that was simmering on top of the barrel heater.

"Sam and Tom should be back soon too." She looked at Stella who was knitting in the corner.

Stella smiled back. "I hope they can bring us some good news", she said.

"The only good news is that someone is fixing this electrical outage." Monica glumly chewed a particularly tough piece of meat. "This is only going to get worse in the spring. I'm afraid George and the motorcycle gang are only the beginning. Right now the cold and snow are keeping most people in one place, but come spring they'll be on the move looking for food."

"No sense coming here, then," Tony answered. "We won't have anything left by then either. Now our propane is gone we'll really be in the dark. How many candles do we have left, Mom?"

"Not many. I think there might be one or two in the storage closet upstairs. Tomorrow we should do a complete inventory of what we have left."

"Don't forget," Stella spoke up from her corner. "We have a whole herd of cows. We might as well eat them as have them freeze or starve to death." Her voice caught. They had worked so hard to keep the farm going, and now it would be all lost.

Tony nodded. "Yeah, we'll have to discuss that when Sam comes back."

Wearily he stood. They hadn't bothered with any candles and only the flickering firelight lit the room. Outside the darkness pressed against the windows. He peered out, hoping to see the travellers coming down the driveway. Nobody. He sank back down into his easy chair.

"I'm getting too old for this adventure." He thought, even as he gave a reassuring smile to the women. Monica finished her stew and quietly pushed her bowl aside. Irma poured them each a cup of hot water from the kettle on the heater. Nobody wanted to talk anymore so the only sound was the clicking of the knitting needles.

CHAPTER ELEVEN

They were all dozing in their respective chairs when a banging on the door made them leap up in alarm.

"Don't open the door!" Tony gasped. "See who it is first."

Stella's hand paused just before she released the deadbolt. "Who is it?"

"It's us!" Quickly she flung the door open and to his apparent surprise, threw her arms around her husband.

"Oh, Sam. Come in, quick. You must be frozen. Where's Tom?"

"We need to put the horse inside first." Sam's eyes barely showed over a frost-covered scarf. "The poor girl is exhausted."

Tony was shaking his hand enthusiastically. "You are a sight for sore eyes."

"Of course, of course. You can put the horse in the old barn. But we have nothing to feed her."

"I have a few oats I took from the barn this morning. Tom is putting her in now. It's cold in there, but at least it's out of the wind".

Catching sight of Irma standing behind her husband, Sam asked. "Do you have a basin or tub or something that would hold water?"

Her forehead puckered. "There should be an old washtub in the shed. Tony, you could go and dig it out."

"Don't be silly. I'm already dressed. I'll find it." And Sam turned, shouting over his shoulder to be heard above the wind that had risen in the night. "You go in and keep warm. We'll be in as soon as we get Star settled."

The horse had been rubbed down and covered with an old blanket, and the returning adventurers were enjoying a bowl of hot stew.

Tom looked around the dim room. "Where's Adnan?"

"There's quite a story there." Monica glanced at her mother-in-law. "Suffice it to say, he and Jason have gone on a rescue mission."

After the story had been told, Sam looked at his meek wife. "I wouldn't have thought you had the guts to do that."

She glanced up from her knitting. "Neither did I." She answered. "Turns out you can do anything if you're pushed hard enough."

"So, what did you find out?" Tony asked impatiently.

"Nobody was there," Sam said quietly. He spooned a mouthful of stew into his mouth. "The town looks all boarded up and the police station was deserted. If anybody was hiding in the houses they didn't come out even though we knocked on a few doors and stood in the street and hollered."

Tom added, "Poor Star was cold and exhausted but we had no place to put her so we had to bring her home with us."

"I wonder where everybody was," Irma said. "They can't all have left and we haven't seen many people passing by here."

"Maybe they all went to a bigger place, thinking there would be more resources." Sam shrugged. "Remember we had a couple of months in the fall when it would have made sense to move south if you didn't have what we have here…gardens, animals and heat."

"Not to mention water", Monica added. "Even if the tap quits, most old farms have a well on the property, and there's the creek here."

"Speaking of farms", Stella spoke up. "How are things at our farm? We were thinking today that we need to butcher a cow or two before they all freeze to death."

Sam, pushed back his chair. "Now that was a surprise," he said. "Tom and I went sneaking into the barn to saddle Star and it's all neat and tidy in there. The horses had hay and even the couple of chickens we left are still alive. While we were leading the horse out, one of the guys saw us and came out. He didn't look quite so fierce as when we saw him here. Turns out under that beard there was a nice young man who thanked us for turning our home over to them."

Tom interrupted, "He said the cows are pretty cold out in the field and of course all the grass is under snow, but they have been keeping an eye on the animals. One of them knows about butchering, so they won't starve."

"I think they're fine over there," Sam added. "They poked a hole in a wall for a stovepipe and set up the old airtight heater we had in the chicken house. They're warm and fed, and that's all they wanted."

"I'm so glad," Stella said. "I was afraid they would destroy everything. And now we know we don't have to sneak around over there."

"Now all we have to worry about is Jason and Adnan getting home safe." Irma got up and poured more hot water into their cups. "We should probably go to bed and get a good night's sleep. Tomorrow we have to decide what to do about accommodating a possible new family. I don't know where we will put them. We're bursting at the seams now."

"Well, if we have to, we can put beds in here." Tony waved around the dark living room. "It's really the only place left in the house except for the kitchen."

"At least the upstairs stays sort of warm from the chimney. But you're right, we might have to turn the living room into a "living" room until spring."

Monica picked up her sleeping baby and began to move towards the stairs. "I probably won't sleep a wink, wondering if Jason is being hit over the head," she said. "But let's go to bed anyway."

"I'll build up the fire," Tony said, moving to do just that. "Sam and Tom must be exhausted, and we have to take the horse back in the morning, too."

It was nearly noon the next day when Monica opened the door to five cold and hungry people. She threw her arms around her husband, then stepped back quickly.

"You're freezing," she exclaimed. "Get in here."

She started undressing the small boy who accompanied the group, crooning the whole time. "Oh, you poor thing. I'll bet you're hungry." Rufus woofed softly and ambled over to investigate the newcomers.

"It's okay," Monica patted the dog when she noticed the boy draw back. "Rufus is just a big teddy bear. He wants to say hi to you."

Shyly the child reached out and petted the furry back. He smiled slightly.

"Come in here." She led the group into the living room where another pot of stew was simmering alongside the kettle of water.

"Sit down." The group sat obediently. So far none of them had spoken, just rubbing their hands together and enjoying the heat.

Monica prattled on while dishing up stew and pouring water into mugs.

"We were so worried", she said. "It's getting colder and we thought it might snow. How far did you have to walk?" She glanced at the silent woman spooning up vegetables. "How old is your boy? What's his name? You must be exhausted. Eat up and we'll find you a bed."

Then she laughed. "I'm sorry. Listen to me. I'll stop talking now."

Jason leaned back in his chair and looked at her smiling. "Where is everybody?" he asked. "I thought there would be a welcoming committee."

"Mom and Dad are lying down with Jack." She answered him. "I don't think they slept much last night. Sam and Stella and Tom went to the farm to return the horse and check on the cattle."

"They didn't get back until late last night – Sam and Tom I mean. The police station and the whole town are deserted and locked up tight, so they didn't find out anything. But they did meet one of the guys at the farm and were pleasantly surprised."

She laughed again. "There I go again. I'm just so glad to see you. I should save some of the news for later."

"Are you done?" she asked the boy.

He nodded shyly.

His mother finally spoke. "He's tired." She said quietly. "Aren't you Ty?"

"It was a long walk," she continued. "And we were already exhausted. I'm Melanie, by the way. I think you met my husband, George, yesterday."

George nodded sheepishly. "Yeah, not under the best circumstances," he said.

"I heard," Monica spoke curtly. Then she turned towards the woman. "We are crowded in here like peas in a pod, but for now you can have a nap in our room. Don't worry about anything until you have slept for ten or twelve hours. You're safe now."

"Come on, Ty." Melanie held out her hand to her son. "Let's go have a sleep."

"I'll find you a nightie." The two women and the boy left the room, leaving the men at the table.

"You need to sleep too, George", said Jason kindly. "We'll give them a few minutes and then you can join them upstairs."

"You're just as tired," George protested. "Sleeping on the floor of an old house isn't exactly relaxing. And then we had the hike back, basically carrying Melanie and Ty."

"Yes, but we hadn't been starving for a month before." Jason answered. "I need to look around and make sure everything is okay here, then Adnan and I will definitely have a lie down too."

Adnan yawned loudly. "I'd be happy to go to bed for a while."

"Not yet." Jason shook his head. "We are going to carry in some more wood and then bring in some more vegetables from the root cellar."

After George had followed his family up the stairs, Monica joined them as they put on boots and coats once more.

"You don't need to come out," Jason told her.

"No, but I need some fresh air." She continued to wrap a scarf around her head until only her dark eyes showed.

Once outside they linked hands and sent Adnan ahead to the woodpile.

"Did you hear about the gun?" she asked quietly.

He looked at her in surprise. "No, what gun?"

"The gun that George used to threaten Mom and Stella with. I came after you yesterday to warn you, but couldn't catch up."

"He doesn't seem the type to use a gun, or to threaten elderly women."

"No, they didn't think so either." She answered. "but your guitar has a big hole in it where Stella bonked him on the head with it."

"Really?" He laughed. "Sounds like they can take care of themselves."

"It's not funny." She rebuked him. "We don't know him and now he's in our house. Who knows what he'll do if he decides we have what he wants?"

"I think what he wanted was food for his wife and kid."

He pulled at the wooden door and they descended into the darkness of the root cellar he had prepared in the fall. Sunlight brightened the first few feet, but the back was in perpetual darkness.

"Let's go and see what we have for food left. I hope it didn't all freeze." He worried. "I didn't have time to dig it very deep."

He cursed as he kicked a rock that lay half buried in the floor. "should've brought the flashlight", he muttered. "what do you see, Monica."

"We're in pretty good shape." She answered. The potatoes and carrots don't seem any the worse for wear. Mom's garden is serving us well."

He rummaged in the dark. "Yeah and I think we have some cabbages back here. It's probably safer in here than in the house. All the stuff in the pantry is freezing."

Monica laughed. "And don't forget the jars of sauerkraut she has hiding under her bed. If we have beef and these vegetables, we should be okay for another couple of months, and we can always hope the lights come back on."

They both filled their arms with vegetables and vowed to bring a flashlight and a box on the next visit. Thankfully, they climbed back into the daylight. They could see Adnan carrying armloads of wood into the house, and down the drive came Stella, Sam and Tom. Now everybody was home, and for the moment, safe.

CHAPTER TWELVE

Christmas was here. A tree stood in the corner of the crowded living room, not too near the makeshift heater. Tinsel glittered on every branch, brightening the room and making Jack laugh with delight.

The old ornaments had been brought down from the attic. Tony had untangled the lights, grumbling as he was expected to. "Kind of silly," he added to the general complaint, "to put electric lights on a tree when there is no power."

"Now, now," Irma chided him. "Maybe they'll come on and it'll be the best gift of all."

"Yeh, sure." He mumbled. "We can always hope."

Irma smiled at her small grandson who had been permanently confined to the playpen and its pile of blankets. "Kids need Christmas. Don't you sweetheart?". She looked up as Monica came down the narrow stairs and into the living room.

"Did you look up in the attic for some kind of toys for Christmas morning?"

"I did", Monica said cheerfully. "And I found some other things that we can use for Christmas surprises too."

"Like what?"

"Ah, it wouldn't be a surprise if I told you, would it?"

They all laughed and Jack, seeing their smiles, returned them with a wide, toothless grin. He held his arms up at his mother, and she lifted him up.

"He's the reason we need a good Christmas," she agreed with her mother-in-law. They both knew that Tony only grumbled because it was expected. He smiled too and tickled his grandson under the chin.

"Did the boys bring back some meat from the farm?" he asked.

"Yes, they're hanging it in the shed." Monica stepped over the mattress on the floor and sat on the worn couch. "I think they invited the motorcycle gang over for dinner tomorrow, too."

Irma looked around in alarm. "Where on earth will we all fit? With ten of us and six of them, plus two kids, we'll have standing room only."

"We'll have to eat in shifts", Monica said. "They will be missing their families, I'm sure, and it'll be good to have some new faces in here."

"We don't need new faces," Irma answered her. "We need to have a normal life back with FEWER faces in the house."

Tony looked at her with concern. "That's not like you Mother."

"I know, I know." And she sat down on the nearest chair. "But you must admit it's getting a little crowded in here, and we never have any privacy. Since George and Melanie and little Ty came, there isn't a spare inch left to move."

She kicked the mattress that Monica had sidestepped. "Even the living room has become a bedroom."

Tony put his arms around her thin shoulders and gave her a quick squeeze. "I know it's tough on you." He sympathized. "The rest of us at least go outside and get some fresh air, while you are housebound most of the time."

"We'll move everything out of here tomorrow," Monica said. "And we'll have to start the meat cooking tonight and keep the fire burning hot instead of banking it. George and Melanie can keep an eye on it since they are sleeping in here."

"Dad's right, Mom. You're in the house all the time. Why don't you go for a walk right now? The sidewalk is clear and there is nothing for you to do in here for the moment. I'll find your boots." Monica laid the now sleeping baby in his playpen and started to rummage in the coat closet.

"We'll both go." Tony gave her shoulders another squeeze. "It's not too cold today and the fresh air will do you good."

She smiled at him. "I'm sorry I'm complaining, honey. We're lucky to be warm and fed. Lots of people will be having a miserable Christmas."

"Okay, let's go." And a few minutes later they were stamping through the snow, holding hands and laughing like teenagers. Monica looked out the window at them and smiled. "They are quite an inspiration," she thought. "I hope they like the present we have for them."

This was a good time, while everybody was out of the house or sleeping, to bring down the toys from the attic and decide what to give Jack and Ty for gifts. They would have to remain unwrapped since all the paper in the house had been used for fire lighting, but maybe there were some old gift bags or cardboard boxes still hidden somewhere.

The next morning, Ty was awake before the sun. Cautiously he lifted his head, peering over his Dad's broad shoulder at the tree.

"I hope Santa found us," he thought. "Grandma Irma said he would, but with no lights on the tree, how could he?"

He lay back down on the pillow and listened to his parent's breathe. He knew they were worried. He might be only six, but he recognized that things were not as they should be. First, the power had gone out. Then his mom and dad stopped going to work. It had been cold in the apartment and he noticed that his mom wasn't eating anything at mealtime.

When his Dad had said they would have to leave and go find something to eat, his mom had cried. But after a long...long walk, here they were, warm and toasty beside the fire in Gramma Irma and Grampa Tony's house. He wasn't sure who all the rest of the people in the house were, or why he had never heard of these grandparents before, but as long as Mom and Dad were close by and he was warm, things were good.

And there were gifts under the tree. He could see them more clearly now as the sun rose and the room began to brighten.

His dad turned over to face him and the bushy beard tickled his face. He giggled.

"Santa came."

"He did?" George looked towards the tree. "Wow! He did find us. I told you he would."

"Can I open presents?"

"Now listen, son." George hesitated. "Santa's power is out too, so there might not be all you wanted under that tree. So, don't be too disappointed, okay?"

"I won't." Ty wiggled happily. "It's Christmas, Dad."

"Of course it is." George stood up and pulled on the pants he had left on the floor beside him. "I'll check the fire. You stay here and keep warm. We have to wait for everybody to come down before even looking at the presents."

"But wait," he said in mock surprise. "Here's a stocking beside you, and I think it has your name on it."

"Really?" the boy squealed and sat up straight, letting the blankets fall to his waist. "Can I have it, Dad?"

The next few minutes were spent emptying the stocking that his mother had fashioned from an old curtain. When the others drifted into the room for their morning cup of hot water, he was anxious to show off his treasures.

"A brand new pencil and notebook." He laid it on the table. "A matchbox car and a pocket knife."

He grinned his gap-toothed smile. "There's even some candy." The adults all smiled indulgently at him. Irma was glad she had found the old box of Christmas candy in with the decorations. She didn't know how old it was, but candy didn't go bad, did it?

Jack also got a stocking with a pair of mittens knitted by Stella and the lone candy cane that been unearthed.

"We'll open gifts after breakfast and chores," Tony ruled. "The motorcycle gang will be over about one and we'll have dinner with them and a little party."

"Stew for breakfast, again." Irma looked around the crowded room. "And let's clear everything out of here except the table and chairs." She looked sternly at George. "Did you keep that fire burning so the two roasts cooked? Twenty pounds of meat takes a long time."

He nodded. "Yes, ma'am. I wouldn't let you down."

"Okay then. We'll start the vegetables so they will be ready when we want to have dinner."

She sighed. "No turkey, I'm afraid, but I did find an onion to add to the potatoes and carrots we usually have."

"And," she added, "there's always sauerkraut." Everybody groaned.

"No moaning," Tony said firmly. "We are all together, we are warm and it's Christmas."

"And Santa came." Ty crowed.

"Yes, he did!" They all smiled at the boy and raised their mugs in a toast. "Merry Christmas everybody." Said Tony.

CHAPTER THIRTEEN

"I don't know why we call them the motorcycle gang," Irma whispered to Monica when the knock came on the door.

"I don't know why, either," Monica answered. "Turns out they are a bunch of nice young men who were just looking for food and shelter. Probably the beards," she added.

The house was redolent with the odours of cooking meat, wood fire and too many people packed into a small space. The "gang" had shown up with gifts.

"Sorry, Sam", Rick apologized. "We had to sacrifice two of the chickens for our contribution."

Sam shrugged. "Well, they were just hanging around anyway. It's not like we were getting eggs from them."

"And one more thing..." Mike held out his offering. "It's a cake," There were gasps all around the room.

"I found a bit of flour in the far reaches of the cupboard, and cooked it in the dutch oven on top of the stove."

"Can we open presents now?" Ty pleaded.

"Of course, of course." Tony stood by the tree. "Everybody sit down and I'll play Santa." He began to rummage under the tree. "There's something here that says to Ty, From Santa."

The little boy's eyes shone with anticipation as he struggled to open a large cardboard box. He had been eying that box all day and could hardly wait to see what it was.

"A sleigh!" he crowed.

His mother looked gratefully at Jason. She had seen him patiently cleaning and polishing the old sleigh that used to be his. "You have to share with baby Jack, I think," she told the little boy.

"Jack's pretty little, yet," Monica said. "I think that sleigh will be yours, Ty."

Everybody had pitched in to make sure there were gifts for all. Stella had been knitting mittens for weeks and everybody got a pair. Sam had dug through his barn and found some snowshoes that were perfect for Jason and Monica. Tony presented Irma with a small wood carving and Irma gave Monica a pair of antique earrings that had belonged to her mother. George and Melanie each received a package of badly needed, almost new, socks and underwear. The two young men, Tom and Adnan each received one of Tony's hunting rifles, complete with ammunition.

"I've never had a Christmas present before," Adnan whispered to Tom.

"I've never had a gun before," Tom answered, stroking the barrel lovingly.

"That comes with shooting lessons," Tony said sternly. "And there is no more ammo so you have to be very careful what you use it for."

They both nodded silently, their grins showing how pleased they were.

After a hearty meal of chicken and beef stew, topped off with the slightly flat cake, they all felt that Christmas had been a perfect day.

"But wait," Jason told his parents. "I have one more gift for you".

"What could it be?" Jason disappeared up the stairs and came back carrying his guitar.

"Isn't that broken?" George looked sheepishly at the floor.

Jason turned the guitar over to show the plywood bottom. He had patched the hole and restored his beloved instrument to working condition.

"I have a song for you." He ducked his head bashfully. "Monica and I wrote it. There wasn't any shopping mall, and we wanted to give you something special."

His fingers brushed the strings and he began to croon:

"Momma and Daddy sitting on the stoop

Waiting for sunset years.

Watching the days and the nights go by

Waiting for kids to come home.

Momma and Daddy gave them their lives

And now they are left all alone."

His fingers began to move faster as the tempo increased:

"Momma and Daddy smiling and happy

The family is gathered around

Watching the days and nights go by

Waiting for lights to come on.

Momma and Daddy gave them their lives

And now the loving comes home."

When he had finished, there was a moment of silence. Irma brushed tears from her eyes and Tony grasped her hand. Then there was applause.

Comments flew around the musician's head.

"Wow!"

"Great job"

"The best gift of the day."

"Monica wrote the words." He protested. "I just put it to music."

"Well, it's wonderful." Irma reached up to hug her son. "It's a gift I will treasure forever." She held out her hands to the room. "This could have been a miserable day," she told the group. "Instead we have all come together, made some new friends, and found out what we can do with very little. I think we should all bow our heads and thank God that we are here, warm and safe, with full stomachs and happy hearts."

After a short prayer, the visitors began to make their way to the door. They shook hands with the men, hugged the women and gave Ty a pat on the head.

When they had gone out into the winter night, the room seemed almost spacious.

"Let's clear up and put the mattresses back in here," Irma ordered. "There should be hot water in the kettle, but we'll need more wood. Then this momma is off to bed. It's been a long and exciting day."

She smiled down at George and Melanie's small son. "Tomorrow your daddy can take you for a sleigh ride." She told him.

Everybody was glad to comply and soon the house settled into darkness. George and Melanie with their boy between them, snuggled on the mattress on the floor. Upstairs, Jason and Monica bundled Jack into his crib and after a few whispered endearments, fell quickly asleep. The two older couples, covered with extra quilts, gave each other a quick peck on the cheek and prepared for sleep.

In the attic, close to the chimney, Adnan and Tom fingered their new guns and whispered excitedly about shooting lessons and hunting.

On his mat in the kitchen, the old dog, Rufus, lifted his head and growled softly. His ears perked up and he padded to the kitchen door. He whined and scratched at the door, then laid down with his nose pressed against it.

CHAPTER FOURTEEN

It was late the next morning when the family began to drift into the living room. George and Melanie rolled up the mattress and built up the fire in the heater. The kettle steamed cheerfully from its accustomed spot.

George peered through the window at the thermometer. "It's only minus 18," he told his young son. "I think we can take that new sleigh out for a test drive."

"Will you pull me, Dad?"

"Of course. Even though we're in the mountains, there aren't a lot of tobogganing hills around here. We'll have to use manpower." George flexed his muscles. "I think there's enough power to pull you."

"Yeah!" The boy scampered to the closet. "Let's go right now."

His father laughed. "Let's eat first." He said. "I'll need my strength for all that hard work."

"Stew again." Said Monica as she filled bowls and passed them around the table.

"We are running low on vegetables." She told Jason. "Yesterday kind of finished off what we have in the house. We'll need to bring in more from the root cellar."

"I'll do that." He said around a mouthful of meat. "And then maybe we can take the boys out for a shooting lesson." The teenagers glanced at each other and grinned.

"And then, we'll bring some more wood from the bush," Jason added. "It'll give us a chance to try out the snowshoes too. They might come in very handy before the winter is done."

"Make sure you shoot away from the house." His mother admonished. "And make sure you know where everybody is so you don't shoot one of us."

"Well, Mom. We won't shoot you since you don't go outside much these days." Her son teased.

She laughed. "If I could reach you, I'd give you a smack." She teased back. "Anyway," she looked at her husband who was across from her at the table. "Maybe this would be a good day to go and see how the Dennis family is doing. It's a nice day and it would be neighbourly at Christmas."

"Good idea." He answered. "Maybe Sam and Stella would like a walk too. If we leave right away we can be back before dark."

"No", Sam answered. "I'm going over to check on the horses. The motorcycle gang..." and he laughed at the nickname..." are doing their best, but they are city boys at heart and not always aware of what's going on outside."

"They make a great cake, though." He pushed back his chair and rubbed his flat stomach. "Even without sugar, it tasted pretty good."

"Stella?" Tony looked at her expectantly.

"I think I'll stay here and look after Jack," Stella answered. "That way, Monica can go out with the boys. Melanie and I can cut up the vegetables when Jason brings them in."

"Okay." Tony stood up. "Come on, Mother. It's you and me and Rufus, I guess." He looked around the room. "Say, where is Rufus anyway? He's usually right under Jack and Ty at mealtime."

"I let him out before the sun was up." George looked out the window. "He shot out of here like a cannon and I haven't seen him since."

"Well, he needs to eat if we're going on a walk." Tony opened the back door and began to call the dog. "That's funny," he said to himself. "He usually comes running." He whistled again but there was no answering bark.

Everybody was bundling up to go outside, so he joined them in pulling on his boots and hooded parka. "You wait here," he told his wife. "I'll find Rufus and then we'll go for our walk."

Outside, they all began to whistle and call. Ty's piping voice mingled with the deeper ones of the men and Monica's shrill whistle.

No dog came running around the barn, or from the trees and Tony began to worry out loud. "Where could he be? He's too old and slow to go very far, and he ALWAYS comes when I whistle." He kept walking towards the barn. Maybe the silly old thing had got himself trapped in there. It had happened before when he nosed the door open, and it closed behind him. Funny he didn't bark though.

"Dad, Dad, come quick." Jason's shout cut through his thoughts.

Tony turned and ran towards the root cellar. The door was flung open and Jason was struggling to carry something through it.

"Oh my God. What happened to Rufus?" Tony gasped as he caught sight of the bundle.

"He's been hurt! Hurry, let's get him into the house."

Gently they laid the injured dog on his mat in the kitchen. Irma hurried off to find bandages. Blood was seeping through his thick fur, forming a puddle under him.

Tony held the large head and crooned to his friend of fifteen years. "What happened?" Monica rushed in with the two boys behind her.

Jason looked up from where he was probing the dog for the source of the blood. "I don't know, but it looks like he was stabbed. And I think the root cellar is empty. All the vegetables we had there are gone."

"Gone!" Irma handed him a basin of warm water. "What do you mean gone?"

"Gone." He started to wash the dog's wound. "I found old Rufus on the floor bleeding and the door wide open. Someone helped themselves."

By this time the entire household, except Sam, was in the kitchen listening in stunned surprise.

"But what will we do?" Stella sat down on the nearest chair and put her hand over her eyes in despair. "Who would do such a thing?"

"Someone hungry." George pulled his son closer to himself. "And desperate."

He looked around at his new friends. "I was lucky that I got bonked on the head before I could do something more foolish. I think we should go after Sam, "he added. "We don't know who is out there or what they will do. He shouldn't be walking alone."

"We'll go!" Adnan grabbed Tom by the arm. "C'mon, let's go bring Sam back." He held up his new rifle, "We can take these for protection."

Irma looked up, her eyes snapping. "Don't you go shooting those things," she admonished. "That won't help, and chances are you'll just shoot yourself in the foot."

"Don't worry. We'll just show that we have them and that should be enough." The door closed firmly and the boys were gone.

Irma began to gently clean the wound on the dog's side. His eyes opened and he looked up at his master, then with a sigh, he sank back into unconsciousness.

"Don't worry, boy," Tony soothed. "We'll soon have you right as rain."

Jason bent over his mother's shoulder. "It looks like someone stuck a knife in him." He said. "I'll bet he ran at them and they just stuck out their knife for him to run into."

"I don't think so." His mother said sharply. "He's wounded on the side. If they just stuck their hand out, he would have been hit in the head or shoulder."

George nodded. "I think I'll go out and see what I can find around the root cellar. They must have left tracks in the snow."

"I'll go with you." Jason stood up. "You're right about one thing. None of us should go out alone until we know the coast is clear. If they will stab a dog, no telling what else they'll do."

The two men left the house and made their way through the yard, careful not to disturb any footprints that weren't their own. Irma and Tony continued to minister to Rufus.

"What about my sleigh ride?" whined Ty. "Did Dad forget?"

"Don't worry," Melanie put her arms around the boy. "You'll get your ride, just maybe not today." She gave him a little pat on his backside. "Go take your coat and boots off and we'll play a game or something."

"Aww. I wanted to go outside."

"Do as I say," she spoke harshly. "Can't you see that poor Rufus has been hurt? Gramma and Grampa don't need you causing a fuss right now."

"He's only little." Stella laid her hand on Melanie's arm. "It's tough being stuck inside with a bunch of old people all the time."

"I think Rufus will be okay." Irma struggled to her feet as Stella took the blood-stained basin of water from the floor and poured it down the sink. Tony continued to stroke the dog's head. "It's a cut, and he must have got a knock on the head. That's why he's still unconscious." She continued.

The five of them looked down at the dog and the man on the floor. From the living room, they heard the baby whimper from his playpen.

"I'll get him," Melanie said. "And then Ty and I can play a game. Try to distract him and myself". Soon they could hear her explaining the finer points of solitaire to her son.

"I thought it was only a computer game." He said and everybody smiled despite their own anguish.

Irma and Tony were moving the old dog to his bed in the corner when Jason and George knocked the snow off their boots and came back into the house.

They both looked grim.

"There were more than two people out there," Jason told them. "It looks like they were moving all the food onto some kind of sleigh or wagon."

"Yeah." George agreed. "The root cellar is completely cleaned out. Rufus must have heard them and he ran over there as soon as I opened the door this morning."

Tony's mouth formed a thin line. "He wouldn't be able to hurt a fly." He said. "All they had to do was pet him and he would have helped them carry stuff. They didn't have to hurt him."

"I'm just glad they didn't try to come in the house," Irma added. "We were all so tired from Christmas we slept right through any ruckus they made." She looked towards the sleeping dog. "I wonder why Rufus didn't bark."

"I wonder who knew we had food stored?" Jason added. "The door was hidden in the snow and we hadn't been out there for a couple of days so there were no tracks." He sat down and put his head in his hands. "I noticed the snow was all messed up this morning, but I was more concerned about the dog than paying attention to that."

"You don't think it was someone we knew, do you?" Irma covered her mouth in dismay. "Why would they do that?"

"I don't know, Mother." Tony shook his head. "People do strange things when they're desperate."

In the corner, the old dog stirred and lifted his head just as Adrian, Tom and Sam banged the door open and stepped inside.

They all spoke at once.

94

"How is Rufus?"

"What happened?"

"Is everything okay?"

"I'll get Rufus some water," Irma spoke loudly. "You all go into the living room and discuss this."

They all trooped out of the kitchen, Tony last of all, after giving a worried glance at his pet.

"Let's have pretend tea and discuss what we should do." Monica met them at the table with the kettle in her hand. They all took their accustomed seats around the scarred table. Ty and Melanie pushed their cards to one side and accepted cups of hot water.

"Even I can have 'pretend' tea," Ty told the assembled family importantly.

After explaining the situation, Jason leaned back in his chair and sipped at his mug. "The question is," he said, "what do we do now? Should we follow them and try to get our food back, or what? This leaves us in a bad situation. They took all our stores."

"It might be dangerous to follow them." George looked back at his new friend. "Do we want to risk getting hurt?"

"Do we want to risk starving?" Jason replied.

"I think we should fight," Adnan said and Tom nodded in agreement. "It's our stuff they took. We worked hard digging that root cellar and putting everything in it."

The older men nodded. "But," said Tony. "What does fight mean? If one of us gets hurt, there is no doctor or medicine to fix him." He looked steadily at the boys. "It's bad enough that we almost lost Rufus. He's a dog. It would be unthinkable to lose a person."

"Somebody knew the food was there," Jason said grimly. "There was just enough to get us through the winter. Now there is nothing."

Sam spoke up. "There's still the farm. The cattle are surviving so far, so we have meat."

"And there's still the sauerkraut under my bed." Irma reminded them. "It'll last for a while." She took her place at the table and sipped the hot water Monica had poured for her.

"What about wild meat?" Stella asked. "When we were kids we lived on deer and pheasant."

"I still think we should go and get our stuff back," Tom said stubbornly. "The guys at the farm will help us."

"Maybe they are the ones who took it," Monica said to him. "Did you think of that? They know we have vegetables and they were here yesterday, so they could have waited until we went to sleep and just helped themselves."

"That would make sense." Tony agreed. "Rufus wouldn't have barked at them if they never left."

Stella shook her head, and Irma looked shocked.

"I can't believe that." She said. "They know we would share what we had. Why steal when all they have to do is ask?"

"Well, who else knows about the cellar?" Jason asked her.

"Anybody could have watched us walk out there and open the door. We don't have armed guards around us."

Tom and Adnan glanced at their guns leaning against the wall beside the kitchen door.

"Maybe we need to be more alert," Tom said. "As people get hungrier in town, they are going to be spreading out looking for food."

Jason pushed back from the table and stood up. "I'm going to follow those tracks," he said. If they go somewhere close by, we'll have the culprits. I won't confront them, but I need to know."

"I'll come with you." George stood also, closely followed by the two teenagers.

"Sam and I will wait for you here." Tony remained sitting. "We're too old to go traipsing through snowbanks. And I want to keep an eye on Rufus."

"I still need to check on the horses," Sam said. "Monica, can you come with me? We don't have to see the motorcycle gang at all. We'll just go straight to the barn."

Jason stopped at the door. "I don't want you going, Monica. We can't both leave the baby."

She started to protest, but Melanie jumped up. "I'll go with Sam." She said firmly. "I haven't been out of this house since we got here, and I need some fresh air." She held up her hand when her husband began to speak. "No, George. I need to pull my weight here. It's perfectly safe at the farm and Sam will look after me. Won't you, Sam?"

"Of course I will," he agreed hastily. "Do you know anything about horses, Melanie?"

"No," she said. "I'm a city girl through and through. But I can help you look at them can't I?"

"Can I come?" Ty asked eagerly, already halfway to the door and his discarded boots. "I can help look too."

Melanie looked doubtful, but Sam nodded, so she agreed. "You can have your sleigh ride after all." She told him.

"Just be careful." Monica helped Ty with his boots. "Do what Sam says and keep an eye open for anything unusual. And come back right away, because we'll be worried about you every minute."

When the house was quiet, Tony grimly checked on the dog, then climbed the stairs to the attic. He moved slowly around the two mattresses parked next to the chimney towards an old trunk under the eaves.

When he returned to the kitchen, he carried an antique revolver with a box of shells.

"Where did you get that?" Monica looked up from where she was reading a battered copy of "Little Women".

"I have my secrets." He smiled back at her. "This was my Grandfather's gun. It's so old, it's never been registered and I don't know if it will still shoot, but at least it looks threatening. This plus the pistol that George was carrying might make us safer."

"George's gun wasn't loaded." She pointed out.

He held up the box of shells. "Aha!" he said. "Look what I found tucked away in my stash. I think these might work."

Interested in spite of herself, Monica came over and examined the old revolver. She nodded. "I hope we never need to use anything like this," she said. "but it's a strange new world we're facing. I mean who knew that I would be talking about going hunting for Bambi? ME!" and she pointed to her own chest. "I didn't even like to see guns on TV, and now we might have to depend on them."

"Yep." Tony was rummaging around in the bottom cabinet. "Where did Irma hide that damned gun?"

"What gun?" Irma was coming from the porch with an arm full of wood.

"George's gun." Tony reached back in the cupboard. "Here it is."

"It doesn't have bullets." She dropped the wood in the wood box and lightly stroked Jack's head as she passed.

"It does now." Monica held up the box of shells. "At least we hope it does. And even empty it might be enough just to wave it around and look threatening."

"Where did you find Grampa's old gun?" She looked with amazement to where it lay on the kitchen counter. "I thought we threw that away years ago."

Tony winked at her. "I have my secrets," he told her. "I couldn't bear to destroy such a beautiful thing, so I hid it along with this box of shells in the attic."

"You would be in such trouble," His wife gave him a scornful look, "If things were different."

In the corner, Rufus groaned and the old couple quickly knelt at his side. "Are you okay, boy?" Tony said softly. "Mother, get him some water, will you?"

She pushed the still full water dish closer to the dog's muzzle. "He's waking up, I think." She said.

And indeed, the dog opened both his eyes and lifted his head. "No, no. Lay down. Stay here." He told the dog, and obediently he laid his white head back down on the floor.

"How can he drink the water if you won't let him lift his head?" Irma asked logically. "It's better to encourage him to stand so he doesn't stiffen up too much."

"I agree." Monica put down the gun she had been examining and knelt beside them. "I'll help you stand him up."

While they were discussing him, Rufus scrambled to his feet as if to show them no help was needed. He began to lap at the water.

"Oh, thank God." Irma stood up and Tony followed suit. They watched as the dog emptied the water dish. "You know," Irma said thoughtfully, "I didn't notice how thin he is getting."

"We're all thin," Monica answered. "We haven't had anything except meat and vegetables for months, and even that's rationed." "And," she continued, "Rufus has been eating the same as us. Not really a doggie diet."

"You're right of course." Irma looked troubled. "I hate to think the dog is hungry, but except for Ty and Jack, we all are."

"I'm not hungry," Tony said. "But I have lost a few pounds." He squeezed his own meagre waist. "But that's a good thing, isn't it? You said I was getting a little chunky."

"Okay," Monica moved towards the living room. "Rufus is looking pretty good so let's have some pretend tea while we wait for the others to come back. Then we can try out these old guns and see if they work."

CHAPTER FIFTEEN

The living room was cloaked in shadows when they finally heard the stamping of boots on the front porch. Tony rushed to open the door.

"It's Sam and Melanie." He said over his shoulder.

"Oh, thank goodness." Stella put down her knitting and leaned forward on her chair.

"Are the men back yet?" Melanie shook off her own coat and then bent to help her small son with his boots. The others shook their heads and her shoulders drooped.

Ty broke in excitedly. "I'm really cold." He told them. "But I didn't complain or cry once. Did I Mom?"

"No, you were a very good boy." She answered.

Sam followed them into the house and set a large package on the floor. "He was a good, brave boy." He affirmed. "The horses are all warm and as healthy as can be expected on a diet of straight hay. Luckily the boys had some meat all butchered when we got there, so we brought back a good-sized piece."

"I thought you wouldn't see them?" Stella asked.

"Mike heard us in the barn and came out to say 'hi'," Melanie explained. "They were as shocked as we were about the theft, and he put together this package for us. Luckily we had the sleigh so we could carry a lot."

"Good." Irma picked up the box with difficulty and started towards the kitchen. "Come and help me get some cups, Ty and we'll have some pretend hot chocolate to warm you up."

Happily, the boy followed her into the kitchen, chattering about the horses and seeing the 'motorcycle gang'.

When they had left the room and Sam was sitting beside his wife next to the fireplace, he filled them in on the news.

"We have to be careful," he told them. "The boys think someone tried to break into the barn last night but ran away when Gerry shouted at them. There were boot prints around the doorway too. They went to the school to see if anyone was there but didn't get that far. They met some guy from town. He said everybody is pretty much out of supplies and those that have them aren't sharing." He sighed. "Can't blame them, I suppose. It's still a long time 'til spring and even then, we can't expect food to just appear."

The others were silent, listening to Irma and Ty chatting in the kitchen.

After a moment, Monica spoke up. "If only the power would come back on," she lamented. "Or even if we knew for sure what caused it."

"I know," Stella seldom spoke but now her voice was firm. "Not knowing makes it worse. And a power outage is one thing, but having everything motorized quit is downright scary." Sam reached out and put his age-spotted hand over hers.

She glanced down in surprise, then continued, "And, who's in charge? "We haven't seen any military, or police, or anything since that nice young man on a horse came by a few months ago."

The hand on hers tightened. She set her chin firmly. "No, Sam, I won't be quiet. You don't think I notice things, but I do."

"Of course you do." Irma placed a pot of chopped beef on the barrel heater's flattened top.

"I'll get this cooking," she said briskly. "The men will be hungry when they come back."

"I'm hungry now!" Ty announced. He stared at the pot as if willing it to boil.

Baby Jack began to sob and Monica picked him up from his nest in the playpen. "Jack's hungry too," she told the little boy. "But you both have to wait until it cooks." She began to rock the baby, trying to soothe him as he continued to wail. "Hush, baby," she sang softly to him and his sobs turned into sniffles.

Irma turned away. "I'll cut up some more meat." Tears filled her eyes and she didn't want Ty to see them. "The smaller it is, the quicker it cooks. I do have a bit of salt to add, so that'll help, and we still have the vegetables we brought in before Christmas."

"Anybody want sauerkraut?" There was a collective groan, but Monica stood and moved towards the stairs. "I'll go get a jar. It's a nutritious supplement even if we aren't fond of the taste."

"And," Tony added, "the sooner it's out of my bedroom the happier I'll be. It smells like vinegar up there."

Yesterday felt years away for all of them.

Stella's needles began to click, the only sound in the darkening room. Even Jack had stopped crying and Ty was drifting into sleep on his mother's lap. Sam sucked on an empty pipe and watched the fire. On the stove, the pot of water and beef began to bubble.

The children were fed and put to bed by six o'clock. The old dog had chewed happily on a meaty bone and now snored on his blanket. One candle had been set in the window, but the rest of the house was in darkness, lit only by the fireplace flame.

"I know it's a waste of wood, but it cheers things up," Tony said defensively as he added another log. He peered anxiously out the window.

Sam's eyes were closed and he rocked gently. "They won't come any faster if you keep watching." He observed wryly.

"I know." Tony shuffled the worn deck of cards mindlessly.

Finally, they heard voices and stamping feet on the porch.

"Oh, thank God." Monica jumped to her feet and rushed to the door.

"Don't open it!" Tony was right behind her. "Look through the peephole first and make sure it's them."

Obediently she peeked through the glass, then eagerly flung the door open. The men pushed in, and she threw her arms around her husband. Melanie grasped George's hand and pulled him towards her. For a moment all was confusion as they tried to remove coats and boots, hug the greeters and talk all at once.

Finally, they were seated around the table. The candle had been moved to the middle of the table and Irma had placed steaming bowls in front of the travellers.

"Eat first." Tony raised his hand when Jason started to speak. "Then we can all hear the story."

When they had finished the meal and were sipping cups of hot water, Jason began.

"We followed the tracks," he said. "They were pretty clear. Then we found the sleigh they had used. It's an old wagon with the wheels removed and boards nailed on for runners. We could see there were four or five of them, but obviously, the sled was hard to move, so they abandoned it and took off in three directions. George," and he nodded in his friend's direction," thought it would be better to stay together so we chose the tracks in the middle to follow."

Tom and Adnan squirmed in their chairs, eager to share their part of the adventure.

"We wanted the boys to come back and tell you where we were." Jason continued. "But they were pretty adamant about staying with us."

"Did they leave anything at all in the wagon?" asked Irma, but all four shook their heads.

"Not so much as an empty jar." Jason smiled ruefully. "Anyway, we kept going and it wasn't long before we knew exactly where we were going."

His Dad looked at him and raised one eyebrow. "The Dennis's?"

"Yep. Right to their back door. Their kid is a teenager, about the same age as these guys, and he and some of his friends came up with the idea. They knew about the root cellar because you told Mrs. Dennis back in the fall that you hoped to dig one. And of course, they knew you had a garden."

He shook his head sadly. "They are in bad shape over there. They have five kids and they all look like skeletons. The baby died about a month ago. The poor thing was wasting away and they had no milk to give her. I don't blame their boy for trying to help, but I wish he had just asked instead of feeling like he had to steal."

George interjected. "The Dad was mortified and he offered to return the stuff that his boy had brought home, but we told him he was welcome to it."

"What about the other boys? Who are they?" Monica asked.

"Well, apparently these kids have been hanging around the school. Their families are all in dire straits so just like Tom and Adnan here, they have left home. Unfortunately, instead of finding a nice place like these two did, they have formed a gang of sorts and are raiding around the area. The Dennis boy met up with them and since he knows the neighbours he tells them about likely places."

Irma's eyes filled. "Those poor people." She clasped her hands together. "We should have checked on them. Losing a baby...." Her voice trailed off.

Tony put his arm around her shoulder. To an inquiring look from his wife, Jason whispered to her. "Mom and Dad lost a baby girl to crib death before I was born."

"Oh!" Monica stood up and came around the table to where her in-laws sat. "I'm sorry. I didn't know that."

Irma sat up straighter in her chair. "It was a long time ago." She brushed a tear away. "But I know how poor Flora must feel. We need to go over there when the weather warms up a bit."

Sam spoke up from his seat by the fire. "We have been pretty lucky. We are warm and still have beef on the hoof to get us through the winter. We should tell the guys at the farm to butcher two or three more and take the meat over to the Dennis's."

"What about the other kids?" Melanie asked. "We can't have a gang running around breaking into homes. Somebody is bound to get hurt."

George nodded thoughtfully. "She's right. They're just a disaster waiting to happen."

Tom leaned forward, his elbows on the table. "What about," he began, then hesitated.

"What about if me and Tom went over to the school?" Adnan continued. "Nobody knows us and we can find out what's going on."

The adults all looked doubtful. "It could be dangerous," Jason said.

"There would be two of us," Adnan argued. "They're just looking for food, not trouble. We can find out how many there are, and what they have planned."

George nodded thoughtfully. "It might work. The Dennis boy didn't see you when we were there, so you'll be strangers, and just like them, you've left home and are looking for a safe place."

"I don't like it," Monica spoke up. "Who knows what they might run into over there."

"You need to take something with you," Jason said. "Something they would value so they don't see you as just two more mouths to feed."

Monica glared at him. "You talk like it's a done deal. I don't think we should send these boys out into the cold. In case you didn't notice, it's winter. If a snowstorm comes up they could get lost or worse."

Irma and Stella both nodded in agreement, but the men looked thoughtful and eyed the two boys with respect.

"I think they should do it," Sam spoke up decisively. "We can't just sit and wait for another raid. As they get hungrier and colder, those boys will get braver. I vote we find out who they are and what they are up to before they come knocking down the door."

"I don't know what we can take to give them," Tom said. "They already have all the food, except what Sam brought from the farm."

"How about matches? Or a flashlight?" Tony suggested.

"No, they probably have a fire going in this weather." Jason shook his head. Then his eyes brightened. "I know, how about a gun?"

"A gun!" The others looked at him in astonishment. "Do you WANT us to be killed?"

"Not a working gun," he clarified. "And we won't include ammunition." He turned to his father. "What about that old pistol you had in the attic? I think it's one step above a musket it's so old."

"My grandfather's gun." Tony nodded. "The one I brought down from the attic today. I think it would still shoot, but not without bullets."

"Yep, that could work." He looked at the two teenagers who were getting excited about having a new adventure. "But you couldn't take your own rifles with you. That's just asking for trouble."

"Wait a minute." Irma stood up and put her hands on her hips. "Number one, how can we send these boys out into danger? And number two," she looked at her husband. "That gun is a family heirloom. Your Grandfather used it. And number three," she glared at her son. "How come Jason knew it was up there when you told ME you had thrown it away?"

Tears came to her eyes as she resumed her seat at the table. "No, I won't have it. We'll find another way."

The others looked down at their hands, avoiding her eyes. An uncomfortable silence hung over the room. The grandmother seldom made such adamant statements.

Tony reached over and patted her trembling shoulder. "There, there. You are probably right. We should look at other options."

She raised her eyes and glared at him. "Don't 'there there' me! I have just as much say in this house as anyone else."

"Of course you do." He pulled his hand back as if burned. "I didn't mean…." his voice trailed off.

"I know exactly what you meant." Her fiery gaze matched the candle burning in the centre of the table. "We'll just appease the old girl and do what the MEN decide."

She pointed her finger at Adnan and Tom. "You will NOT go over to that school!" she told them. "It's getting colder outside; it's probably going to snow and I don't want to explain to your mothers someday how we let you get yourselves hurt or killed."

They nodded meekly. Monica covered a smile with her hand.

"Way to go, Mom." She said. "Sometimes it's better to be careful and not go rushing out to save the world."

Jason glared at her, but she only smiled back.

Sam stood up from his seat by the fire and stretched. "It's been a long strenuous day," he announced. "I'm going to bed. Come on, Mother. I need you to keep me warm up there."

Slowly, and by twos, they all left the central room leaving George and Melanie to unfold their mattress and move their sleeping son closer to the fire.

When they were safely snuggled under the pile of blankets, George pulled his wife to him and she tucked her head onto his shoulder.

"What do you think?" he asked her. "Should we just leave those kids at the school alone?"

"No," she answered. "But I think we should be more concerned about feeding them than shooting them. They're like us, wandering around looking for a safe place, but not as lucky as we are right now."

"You're right." He agreed. "I'm ashamed that I came in here and threatened poor Irma. She's tough though." He chuckled. "Those two old ladies got the best of me. When she makes up her mind everybody better listen." He lifted himself up onto one arm. "We'll need to do something. As those boys get more desperate they might come back."

"Well, we have a few days." His wife turned her back and settled down to sleep. "They have all our food so they're better off than we are. It's your turn to put wood on the fire." Her eyes closed and she left him alone with his thoughts.

The old house creaked around him and the only sound was the crackling of the fire. Soon, George too was snoring.

Only Rufus heard the stairs creak and the back door open. He raised his head, but soon relaxed as he recognized Tom and Adnan. He didn't see them slip on their heavy boots and coats and creep stealthily across the yard, each grasping their Christmas present.

CHAPTER SIXTEEN

It was snowing heavily when George got up to put another log in the stove. He peered out into the early morning light, but couldn't see more than a few feet. He shrugged and crawled back into bed, pulling the blanket over his head he drifted back into sleep.

He was brought back to awareness by Ty jumping onto his back. "Morning, Daddy." He crowed. "what can we do today? It's snowing. Can we build a snow fort?"

George rolled over and grabbed his son, pulling him under the blanket with him.

"Easy, Sport." He ruffled the boy's hair. "It might be a bit cold to play outside today. We'll have to see."

"Okay, Dad." Ty could be not be held for long. He jumped up and sat at the table. "I'm hungry." He announced.

George and Melanie crawled from under the blankets and quickly dressed in the jeans and shirts they had left close by the fire. They had barely finished folding up the mattress when the rest of the family began drifting into the room.

Irma glanced at her watch. "It's late." She said. Past ten. We must have all been exhausted." She bustled into the kitchen and returned with a full kettle. "I'll get some stew heated for breakfast," she promised the waiting boy.

Ty wrinkled his nose. "Stew again!"

His mother gave him a gentle slap on the wrist. "It's what we have." She admonished him. "Remember how hungry you were when there was nothing?"

"We're all sick of stew." Sam agreed. "Why don't we try something different?" He grinned at their astonished stares. "You know...like steak! Or pot roast." It's all beef and we don't need to always boil it."

Stella and the rest nodded. "You're right, Sam. We've been stewing it because that seemed the best way to cook on this old heater. But we could get the fire burning really hot and fry steaks in the cast iron frying pan."

"I think we should go hunting too," Jason added. "The boys could learn how to shoot those rifles we gave them and even deer meat would be a change at this point."

"I remember setting rabbit and pheasant snares when I was a boy." Said Tony. "They could be roasted on a spit in the fireplace."

Sam nodded. "Yep, I did that too. Boys learned that kind of thing when we grew up."

"Okay then." Jason stood up. "I'll get those boys out with their new guns as soon as this storm is over." He left the room and they heard his footsteps ascending the stairs.

Irma called up the stairs to him. "Let them sleep." She told him. "They can't go outside in this weather, and as long as they're sleeping they're not hungry. I wonder if he heard me?" She added to herself, then smiled at the thought of the two teenage boys and how much they could eat if left to it.

"Can I have an apple?" Ty asked innocently.

"Now, you know there are no apples or cookies or bread." His mother admonished him. "We have pretend hot chocolate and meat, and we're very lucky to have that. Or" and she grinned mischievously, "you could have sauerkraut."

Irma laughed at the look on the boy's face. "Yes, we are lucky. But now I'm even more worried about the Dennis family. Apparently, they are much worse off than us." She looked out at the blowing snow. "At least they are warm and have water."

"They have some food now too," George said glumly. "Ours." A sheepish look crossed his face. "I mean, yours. We are just lucky enough to be able to share the product of your work."

Monica put Jack into his playpen, then stood looking down at him. "I'm worried too. This is no diet for a baby. He should have milk."

Suddenly she looked at Sam, her eyes bright. "What about your cows, Sam? Aren't they dairy cows? Don't dairy cows give milk?"

"They do," he said slowly. "But first they need to have a calf, and there won't be any calves this year." He looked around the table. "We don't have a bull on the farm," he explained. "Too much trouble. All our cows are bred by artificial insemination and of course, there was none of that last fall."

"Besides," he added. "We've turned them all out in the pasture so they are half wild. Trying to catch one to milk would be a nightmare, and most of them will have dried up by now. They have to be milked regularly to keep producing."

"They're catching them to butcher," Monica argued. "Can we at least try? Jack and the Dennis kids need more than meat."

Sam and Tony glanced at each other and shrugged.

'We can try." Sam acceded. "But I don't want to give you false hope. It's one thing to butcher, it's quite another to try to touch them. And remember, they are milked by machine, so wouldn't be accustomed to the hand method." He flexed his fingers thoughtfully. "I don't even know if these old hands would be strong enough anymore."

Tony laughed. "I'm told it's like riding a bike," he said. "All we have to do is find a cow with a calf, who hasn't dried up, tie her up and pull on her teats. Easy as pie." He smiled at Monica. "I know Jack needs this." He assured her. "We'll try, Honey."

While they were talking, they heard footsteps rapidly descending from upstairs. Jason almost ran into the living room, red-faced and breathing hard.

"They're gone!" He shouted at their shocked faces. "Those kids packed up their stuff and sneaked out in the night. And worst of all, they took their guns."

"Why would they do that?" Stella asked. "Where do you think they went?"

"Trying to be heroes." Jason sat down heavily. "We should never have mentioned going to the school." He waved towards the snow beating against the window. "And to go out in this. It's not only dangerous, it's also foolhardy!"

George pounded his fist on the table, causing the others to jump. "Damn kids. Now we have to go find them and all of us are in danger!"

"You are not going out in this." His wife said firmly.

"I agree," Monica said. "They will have to take their chances until the storm passes."

Jason stood up and began to pace in the small space between the table and the heater. He scowled, failing to notice his baby son watching him with quivering lips. Ty too, watched him, eyes round with astonishment and fear.

Jack began to whimper and Monica scooped him up. "Sit down, Jase. You're upsetting the babies."

"I'm not a baby!" Ty protested as he moved closer to his mother's side. "Is Tom and Adnan in trouble?"

Melanie gave him a quick hug. "Yes, they are." She answered. "But you are not. They are being very silly and Daddy and Uncle Jason are angry at them."

"As are we all." Tony agreed. "But we simply can't do anything right now. All we can hope is that they find shelter and don't do something stupid." A smile played at the corners of his mouth. "More stupid."

Jason stopped pacing and pulled a chair closer to the heater. "Give me the baby," he told Monica. "We'll wait until the storm passes, then decide what to do." He began to play with a stuffed toy, holding it up for his son to see. Soon they were both giggling, while the rest of the family settled into their various pursuits.

Irma poured more water into the kettle for dishwashing. Monica and Melanie read and Stella took up her knitting. The men and Ty took out the battered deck of cards and a crib board. The wind howled outside the doors, but they were snug inside. All of their thoughts were with the two boys and what they might be facing in the next few hours.

CHAPTER SEVENTEEN

The storm continued for three more days. Jason paced until his mother and wife pointed out to him that he was making things worse.

The meat that Sam had carried from the farm was almost gone and they almost gagged when confronted with another bowl of 'stew'. As the supply dwindled, Irma added more water hoping to make it stretch further. Everybody ate less so the baby and six-year-old would not be hungry. Rufus became more lethargic as his body tried to heal without fuel. They could only allow him a small portion once a day.

Finally, on the third day, as he dumped an armload of wood into the box, Sam said, "I think it's starting to lift. The wind isn't as fierce and I could see all the way to the barn."

Every head lifted at the news. George peered out the window. "I think you may be right, Sam."

Jason began to pull on his boots. "Good! I'm going to find those boys. And when I catch up to them, I'm going to give them both a good hiding for scaring us."

"Don't go." Monica laid her hand on his arm as he reached for his coat. "It's slowed down, but it hasn't stopped. And it's late. It'll be dark in an hour."

His father agreed. "You are in no shape to go fighting through four feet of snow in the dark. All you'll do is make the rest of us worry about you too. Just wait until morning."

Jason sank into the nearest chair and put his head in his hands. "I feel responsible." He told them. It was my bright idea to send them over to spy on those kids. They saw it as a big adventure and couldn't resist."

"It's not your fault." Monica patted his shoulder. "We all thought it was a good idea until your Mom vetoed it. And nobody forced them to sneak out in the middle of a storm."

"Not the brightest move." Sam nodded. "And they probably didn't even know where they were going. We told them the school, but they don't live around here so how could they know where it is?"

Irma looked at him wryly. "Thanks for pointing that out, Sam. Now I have something else to fret over." Angrily she slammed a bowl in front of Ty. "Eat!" she commanded him.

He looked up at her with wounded eyes. "I'm not hungry, Grandma."

Instantly her anger evaporated. "Oh, Ty." She gathered him into her arms. "I'm sorry, I'm not mad at you. I'm just a bit off-kilter."

Then she felt his forehead and looked across the table at Melanie who was listlessly playing solitaire. "He's burning up, Mel. Are you sick, Ty?"

Melanie looked up in alarm. "He's been restless at night," she said as she came around to take her son's temperature with the back of her hand. "And he's not hungry which is strange. He's always hungry."

Irma stood up. "I have a thermometer somewhere around here. Let's take his temp." She looked at her son who still sat in the same position, with his head in his hands. "And don't you go sneaking out too." She told him firmly. "We couldn't take one more crisis in this house."

Sam and Tony exchanged wry grins. They knew better than to contradict an angry wife. "Are you finished with the cards, Melanie? Maybe we'll have another crib game."

Soon the little boy was tucked under blankets on the sofa. His mother gave him water to sip and his dad sat on the arm of the couch. The thermometer had registered 101 degrees. "Way too high", they all agreed.

The older men played cards and quietly discussed the situation. Hopefully tomorrow they would be able to make a trip to the farm and replenish their supply of beef. Sam was looking forward to seeing the men and bringing up a cut of meat suitable for a steak. He was worried, too, about the horses.

"I hope they were able to get out to the barn and give them some water." He worried to his old friend.

Tony nodded. "Well, two things we all have plenty of are wood and water, so as long as they could open the door it's probably okay." He glanced out at the darkening sky. "At least the snow is quitting, but it'll be a struggle going anywhere."

Jason interrupted them. "If you two go to the farm, George and I can make our way to the school and see if we can find those two juvenile delinquents."

"And on the way, you can check on the Dennis' house," his mother added. "With all those little kids they're worse off than us."

"That's because they're not the gardener you are, Mother." Tony smiled at her. "Your vegetables and canning helped keep us moving for a long time."

She sighed. "And now that's all gone. I hope it helped them." She frowned as another idea came to her. "you know, one thing I was holding on to was that spring would come and we could plant again." Tony nodded as she continued. "But what will we plant? All the seeds were in the root cellar and from what you say, it's completely empty."

Stella looked up from her knitting. "you're right, Irma. I hadn't thought of that. Even if they couldn't be eaten, they will all be frozen by now."

At that moment, Jack began to whimper. Monica began to rock him gently. "He's hungry," she said. "I'll give him the stew that Ty didn't eat."

At the mention of Ty's name, all eyes turned to the family huddled together on the sofa.

"He's still burning up," George said to their inquiring looks. "I wish we had some aspirin."

"There might be some at the farm." Stella said. "Tomorrow when Sam goes over there, he can check."

George nodded. "We'll just have to keep him hydrated and as cool as possible until then."

"Kids get fevers all the time." Irma tried to reassure them. "It's probably just a cold."

The room became silent. Nobody had the energy to light the single candle so they sat in the dark listening to each other breathe. Outside the wind began to die, and by midnight the snow had stopped.

CHAPTER EIGHTEEN

When Jason came downstairs in the morning dressed for hiking, he found George and Melanie awake and hovering over their small son. The boy's face was as white as paper and his breath raspy.

"I can't go and leave them," George told him. "If I go anywhere it'll be to the farm to see if there's any aspirin over there."

Jason nodded. "I understand." He answered. "I'll go alone."

"Oh no, you won't!" Monica had followed him down the stairs. "Nobody should go out of here by themselves."

"What do you suggest?" he asked her. "I can't ask Dad or Sam...it's way too far and too strenuous for them."

"I'll go." She turned back towards the stairs. "I'll tell Mom and she'll watch Jack. Just give me a minute to put on some warmer clothes."

"And eat something." Her voice drifted down the stairs. "We can't go out there without something hot inside us."

He looked doubtfully at George. "I don't know if that's a good idea. What do you think, George?"

He shrugged. "Why not? She's as strong as the rest of us and she's right about sticking together."

By this time everybody was in the kitchen, dressed and ready for the day's activities. "If George is going with Sam," Tony said. "I'll stay here to bring in wood and watch over things."

"I'll put some water and some soup in a couple of thermoses while you eat." Irma busied herself at the counter. "And take extra socks." She said over her shoulder as Monica joined her husband at the table. "There's nothing worse than cold, wet feet."

"Okay, let's go then, Monica." Jason pulled on his boots and peered out the window. The snow had stopped and everything was covered in white. Trees had disappeared under a thick blanket and the land sparkled in the bright sunlight. The outside thermometer registered minus 35C.

"If we don't make it back by dark, don't worry, "Monica instructed her mother-in-law, "we'll go to the Dennis house and spend the night." She kissed her baby boy, patted him on the head, then turned and followed her husband out into the frigid day.

Stella reached out and stroked Ty's hot head. "How is he today?" she asked tenderly.

"Worse," Melanie answered her. "None of us slept much. I sure hope there is some kind of medicine over at your house."

"Why don't you go upstairs and sleep in our room for a while." Stella sat down beside the restless boy. "I'll keep an eye on him."

"Don't worry," she replied to Melanie's questioning look. "I'll call you if he looks like he's getting worse. And I'll see if I can get him to take some broth."

Melanie nodded. "Okay. I won't be much use if I'm falling down." She watched as George and Sam put on their boots and coats. "You be careful," she told them shakily. "We need you back here as quick as possible."

George blew her a kiss. "We'll be back before dark." He told her. "You go have a nap. I'm sure Ty will be better soon."

When the house was nearly empty Irma called Tony into the kitchen. She pointed shakily at Rufus's blanket. "He's not moving." She said tearfully. "I think this was just too much for him." She sank to the floor and began to sob.

"Poor old Rufus. What a way to go, hungry and hurting."

Tony sat down beside her and pulled her close. His voice was shaky as he tried to comfort her. "Poor old boy," he echoed. "But he was old....

120

fifteen this year. He's in a better place, I'm sure." He pulled away from her and tried to smile. "Remember when we got him, all big feet and floppy ears?"

She smiled back. "Yes, and remember when he ate your favourite shoes and chewed the TV stand?"

Just then, Stella came around the corner. She stopped when she saw them sitting on the floor with their arms around each other. Her eyes went to the still form of the old dog.

"Oh, Poor guy. I'm so sorry."

The old couple struggled to their feet. Irma groaned, "I'm too old to be crawling around on the floor," she said. Tony nodded in agreement.

"I guess we'll put him in the shed for now," he said. "In the spring I'll bury him down by the creek."

He struggled to pick up the dog. Stella held the door open and he carried him on to the porch. He would move the body later when he was dressed for the bitter cold.

For a moment he stood over the still form, taking deep breaths and bracing himself to face the family. He had to stay strong, he told himself. They were depending on him.

Jason and Monica stepped out onto the verandah and surveyed the snow covered driveway. It sparkled and shone like diamonds in the bright sunlight. They were both grateful for the sunglasses Irma had found. They shouldered their backpacks and stepped off the porch, immediately sinking almost to their hips.

"This won't be easy." Jason glanced at his wife. "Are you sure you want to come?"

She met his gaze. "I'm not letting you go into potential danger by yourself. At the very least I can run for help."

He eyed the driveway ruefully. "I don't think anybody will run anywhere in this."

"Okay." He stepped forward. "I'll go ahead and break trail and you follow. We'll trade places every fifteen minutes or so." He spoke over his shoulder as she followed. "It's further by road than through the fields, but I'd hate to get lost out there."

She nodded. "Let's just follow the road. Maybe the trees will have kept it from drifting too badly."

Fifteen minutes later they had reached the end of the driveway. The snow on the road was smoothed by the wind, and just as deep as in the yard. The trees on each side would help keep them on track. Sighing, Monica glanced back and saw Sam and George step out onto the porch.

"I hope they find some medicine for poor Ty at the farm."

"I hope they make it to the farm." Jason panted. "It's hard slogging through this snow. I'd suggest waiting a day or so, but I don't see it changing anytime soon."

"You know what we need?" Monica moved into the forward position. "Snowshoes, or skis."

He stopped and slapped his forehead with a mittened hand. "Of course. Remember our Christmas presents?"

"Snowshoes." She looked back down the driveway. "Should we go back and get them?"

"Probably not. By the time we plow back down there and practice walking with them, it'll be afternoon again. Let's just go ahead."

To conserve their energy, they didn't speak as they struggled forward. After an hour they had only covered a quarter of the distance to the Dennis farm. Their faces burned from the biting cold.

"At this rate," Monica took a sip of warm water, "We won't get there until afternoon. We'll have to stay there and set out for the school in the morning."

She tucked the water bottle into an inside pocket of her parka. "I hate to leave Jack that long."

"It'll be easier going home," Jason reassured her. "And Mom and Stella will take care of Jack just fine." He reached out and touched her shoulder. "Ready?"

"Yep, let's go."

Late that afternoon the Dennis farmhouse came into view, giving them the energy to push forward. When the door opened the couple almost fell into the warm interior.

Ervin Dennis stepped back in astonishment at the snow covered apparitions stumbling through his front door. "What the…."

"Oh my goodness." Flora hurried forward. "It's Jason. What are you doing here in this weather?"

"Come in, come in." She began to unwrap Monica's scarf. "Look at you. You're frozen to the bone."

"Get chairs for them." She ordered one of the children gawking from the other side of the room.

The chairs appeared and Jason and Monica sank gratefully into them. Ervin bent and helped them remove their boots and Flora continued unwrapping scarves and unbuttoning coats. Someone handed them cups of hot water which they cradled in their cold hands.

"Thank you." Monica was finally able to say. She glanced at Flora, noticing her diminished size. "Can I use your bathroom?" she asked. "It was a long walk".

"It's the outhouse, I'm afraid." Flora handed her coat back. "Sorry."

When Monica returned, after being escorted to the outdoor facilities by a small girl, she found Jason huddled beside the wood stove in the middle of the room. She stepped over the mattresses that were arranged around the stove and was gently guided to the couch.

When they were all settled around the stove, steaming cups in their hands and wet coats hanging on the wall, Jason was able to ask his questions.

"Our two young guests, Tom and Adnan went out the other night before the storm," he explained. "We think they were going to the school to meet up with the other young people there. Have you seen them?"

"They didn't come here." Ervin shook his shaggy head. "Barry!" he called to the boy who was standing in the corner warily watching their guests.

The boy stepped into the circle of mattresses. "I ain't seen them." He muttered.

"Are you sure?" Jason looked at him. "You've been over to the school. Did you see anybody new hanging around there?"

"Nope." The boy shook his head, keeping his eyes on the floor. His long hair fell over his face, hiding his expression from them all. "I ain't been out of the house since it started snowing."

"For heaven's sake, Barry." His mother said impatiently. "Stand up and look at us when we talk to you. We know you were hanging out with those hoodlums."

She looked over at Jason. "He's right about not being out of the house though. The furthest any of us went was to get snow to melt and wood for the fire."

"Do you know what these people have done for us?" she reached over and grasped her son's thin arm. "You stole their food but they came over here and told us we could keep it. Do you know how close we were to

124

starving?" She gave him a slight shake. "If you know anything at all, you'd better tell them."

Jason said gently, "Their names are Tom and Adnan," the boy's head jerked up as Jason continued. "One is blonde and the other is dark. We're desperate to find them."

"How dark? Like black?" Barry's eyes met Jason's with real fear showing in them.

"More brown than black," Jason answered.

"They better not show up at the school. Those guys hate brown people. They'll kill 'im!"

The adults all stared at him in disbelief.

"What are you talking about?" Flora's voice was shrill. "These kids will kill somebody? Who are they?"

"They blame brown people for the power going out," Barry spoke softly, but desperately. "I didn't know they would hurt anybody. They were just hungry and needed food. I went over there and 'cause I live around here they thought I would know where to find it." He looked directly at Jason. "I didn't want to steal, but they told me if I didn't help, they'd beat me up and burn our house down, and they are MEAN."

Ervin leaned forward in his chair. His face was almost hidden behind a full beard, but his kind eyes shone at his son. "Have you ever seen them hurt anyone, Son? Threatening to beat you up is one thing, but killing them?? Really?"

"They go into town sometimes." Barry moved closer to his father. "They steal what they can find. Once they stole a girl."

"A girl?" they all gasped.

He nodded. "They said that real men need a woman. I saw her at the school, and then she was gone. And I don't think they took her home."

Tears leaked from his eyes. "I've never been back since we took the food from the Baldini's."

"Well, you are going back tomorrow." His father spoke firmly. "We need to know what's going on over there. I thought it was just a bunch of kids banding together for safety. Now it appears that they are actually dangerous." He glanced at his ten-year-old daughter standing silently by the stove.

"You know them and they know you, so you can go in and see if they know anything about those boys."

"I can't go in there." Barry cried. "They don't trust me."

"Don't worry," Jason spoke up. "Monica and I will go with you. All you have to do is show us where they are and we'll do the rest." He turned to Flora Dennis. "I hope you can find room for us to sleep."

She nodded. "We have lots of room. We'll just bring another mattress down from upstairs." She sighed. "We don't have much food left. One more jar of peas and a rabbit that Ervin trapped, but we'll be happy to share. The peas are yours anyway."

Monica patted her hand. "Your kids need those peas more than we do. Besides Irma sent a thermos of soup with us. All we need is sleep. The walk over here was pretty harrowing."

When the men went to get a mattress, Monica studied the room and its inhabitants. Besides Barry, two gaunt little girls and a boy of about four huddled together. Their eyes were huge in their thin faces as they returned her gaze.

She turned to her hostess. "You know, Flora, the teacher in me keeps calling. If this darkness goes on for a long time, we need to educate these kids."

Flora nodded. "I know. We've been treating this as a temporary power outage, but it's way bigger than that. If we live through the winter, we will have to band together and make a future plan." At the mention of living, her eyes filled.

Monica reached over and patted the cold hand. "I'm so sorry about your baby." She said. "We are trying to think of options so the rest of us don't go the same way. Sam and Stella Johnson ran a dairy farm and Sam is going to try to get us some milk. He turned his cows out so we are hoping that one of them might be milkable."

At Flora's hopeful look Monica continued. "We haven't been very good neighbours, I'm afraid. We should have brought you over some of our meat."

"Meat?"

"Yes, we have been butchering the cows so even though we have no bread or anything, we do have meat. Sam and George are going over there today so we'll make sure you get some."

"Well, how could you know?" Flora stood up to help the men move beds and bedding. "We had a garden, but with five kids it went away pretty fast. And I'm not really a canner…usually I just froze things. We have lots of 'stuff'," she looked around the room, "and lots of kids, but I never thought more than two weeks ahead for food. We just ran to the store."

"Yes, I know." The younger woman agreed. "I was the same. That's why we headed for Jason's parents' place. We knew they would have food." She sighed. "Unfortunately, they also have a houseful of people, so it probably wasn't going to last much longer. And now," she sighed, "there is none left."

"What people?" Ervin asked. "Neighbours?"

"No, not really. The Johnson's are there, so they're neighbours. But Tom and Adnan followed us when we came, and then George and Melanie found us when they were looking for a safe place. They have a six-year-old and our baby, Jack is just over a year, so we are bursting at the seams."

Flora shook her head. "And we are the lucky ones. We have wood to burn and water to drink. The pipes froze before Christmas, but the well is still there. In the meantime, we're melting snow. People who live in cities don't even have that. We're out of food now, but the winter is nearly half over."

"We're talking about going hunting too," Jason added to the conversation. "I'm seeing deer tracks around our place. Up to now, we haven't needed to," he glanced at Barry who was listening silently, his head on his chest and his hair covering his eyes. "Things are more desperate now," he added quietly. "That's another reason to check on that schoolhouse gang. We don't need to add another danger to the list."

"I'm making rabbit soup," Flora said. "It's a little thin, but if I add the peas we can call it stew."

"We've got some left in our thermoses." Monica poured their contribution into the pot, and the older woman looked at her with a smile.

After their meagre meal, they joined the family on the mattresses and drifted into sleep. Jason and Monica were exhausted from their day of walking and didn't hear Ervin putting more logs on the fire during the night. The old house creaked in the cold. Outside, a lone wolf began to howl.

CHAPTER NINETEEN

The old farmhouse was silent. Baby Jack slept in his playpen. Ty tossed restlessly under Stella's watchful eye.

In the kitchen, Tony and Irma started to clear the dog's corner. They mournfully picked up his empty food dish, emptied the water down the sink and folded the worn blanket.

A frantic pounding on the back door made them both jump up. Melanie tiptoed down the stairs.

"Who do you think it is?" she whispered.

"Don't open that door," Tony cautioned, "until you see who it is."

Irma had already flung the door open and started to sob with relief. "It's the boys!" She reached out and pulled them in.

"Oh, where have you been?" she scolded even as she unbuttoned their coats. "We've been so worried. Monica and Jason went to look for you. Come in, and take those boots off."

"Melanie," she ordered. "Get these boys some hot water to drink. They look frozen. Stella, see if there is any of that stew left in the pot. Get in here, boys and sit down."

Tony slowly stood and came over to help them remove their winter gear. He took their rifles and placed them carefully in the corner of the kitchen.

"You boys gave us quite a scare." He said softly, studying their weary faces. "you'd better tell us why you snuck out into a storm in the middle of the night, and why we shouldn't just send you back out there."

Freed of their heavy clothing, Tom and Adnan looked very small. They had lost weight, Irma noted, so hadn't been eating. She looked at Tony with a warning in her eyes.

"Let's get them warmed up and fed before we hear their story." She said. "Come on boys. There is only a bit of meat left but you obviously need it."

They all moved into the living room, closer to the fire. Stella put cups of hot water in front of them and Melanie silently spooned watery stew into bowls.

Jack sat up in the playpen, looking with interest at the family. He began to whimper and Irma picked him up and began to rock him gently.

They all watched expectantly as the last spoonful was cleaned from the bowls. Tom sighed and began to tell his story:

"We just thought we'd be able to help." He started. "We knew Mrs. Baldini didn't want us to go, but there's two of us so we decided to go to the school and just take a look around."

"Why did you take your guns?" Tony asked gruffly. "That's just asking for trouble."

"Well, we figured we might need protection. We meant to hide them before we got there."

Adnan took up the narrative: "We don't really know where the school is, so we thought we'd go to where the old wagon is and follow the tracks. But we didn't count on the snow. By the time we got to the wagon we were already tired, so we decided to crawl under it, light a small fire and sleep for a couple of hours." He grinned sheepishly at Tony. "We did remember a few things you taught us like always take matches, and don't carry loaded guns."

"So anyway, that worked. We ripped off some sideboards and lit a fire, crawled under the wagon and dozed off.

"Trouble is," Tom added, "We didn't count on the snow. When we woke up, we were completely covered in it. The wagon kept it from falling on us, so we were in a kind of cave. It was so warm with the fire we were able to take off our coats and put them under us to lay on. We had water and we could hear the storm, so we just stayed there. Then," and he looked rueful, "we realized that with the heat inside and the wet snow, our cave was freezing around us."

Tony nodded. "Of course, that's how they build igloos in the far north. But they build a door into them."

"Yep, but we had no door. And our cave was getting smaller as we pulled boards from the bottom of the wagon for our fire. So, we started poking at the snow, trying to make an air hole."

Adnan piped up. "We were really scared," he said. His voice shook at the memory. "It was getting really tight, so we let the fire go out. We just took turns digging and poking at the ice and snow. You wouldn't believe how hard it was. And we didn't know how deep it was, or if the wind was still blowing, or even if it was day or night."

Melanie was holding her feverish son and now said sarcastically, "Obviously you got out. Here you are"

The boys turned wounded eyes toward her. "Is Ty sick?" asked Tom.

"Yes, he is. He has a fever and we don't have anything for it." She held him close to her breast and began to rock.

"So you got out?" Irma prompted.

"Yeah, we finally got out. We kept falling asleep, but one of us kept poking at the snow and finally we saw light. So, we put on our stuff and came back here. How long were we gone?" Tom asked anxiously. "We lost track after the first day."

"This is day four," Tony told them. "We couldn't go looking for you because of the storm, and everybody was so worried." He reached across the table and grasped their hands. "You have to understand, boys, you are part of this family. We aren't all related by blood, but we have chosen to band together as a family group. When you decide to do something on your own, you have to think of how it will affect the rest of us. You already have families' worried sick about you in the city, and we don't want to have to explain to them someday that we let you do something stupid. You could have died out there, and we wouldn't have known where to look."

"And now," Stella spoke up. "you may have caused Jason and Monica to walk into danger too. They've gone to the school to see if you made it there."

The boys hung their heads. Tony's grasp on their hands tightened.

"I'm sure they will be fine." He assured them. "But I hope you consider the consequences of what you have done. We're not your parents so maybe you don't feel we have any authority, and you think you are big enough to make your own decisions, but adults stop and consider the whole picture before jumping in."

They both nodded. Tears rolled down their cheeks.

"Anyway," Irma stood up briskly. "You both need to go up and sleep and put on clean clothes. We'll heat some water so you can have a good wash too. You both stink."

Everybody smiled in relief.

"Hey, wait a minute." Tom looked around the room. "Where's Rufus."

Tony's face fell and Irma's eyes filled with tears.

"Poor old Rufus just couldn't go on anymore," Tony said sadly.

"He was weak anyway from not enough food, and the injury was just too much."

"He died?" Adnan choked out. "They killed that old dog?"

"Nobody killed him." Tony looked at them. "He was old and weak. He's in a better place now."

"No, they killed him. Those thieves killed him when they hurt him." Tom's voice was grim. "I hope Jason finds whoever did it and gives them a taste of their own medicine."

"Go to bed," Irma said sharply. "Jason is looking for you, not trouble. He'll go to the school, and when you aren't there, he'll come home."

After the boys had left to get a few hours of sleep, Tony stood at the window looking at the furrows in the deep snow left by the trail breakers. "It'll be a long way to the farm," he thought. "They'll have to break trail the whole way." He sighed heavily and went to get his boots. They would need more wood. Tomorrow he would send the teenagers out into the woods to cut some more.

Behind him, he could hear Ty's heavy breathing, the baby whimpering and the women's crooning.

CHAPTER TWENTY

The sun had barely touched the horizon when Jason awoke. For a moment he wondered where he was and why he was sleeping on the floor. Then it all came back to him and he turned his head and observed the Dennis family sleeping around him. As he watched, Ervin stood up and moved to the wood box in the corner.

The clatter of the wood being dropped into the stove woke Monica and she blinked in his direction. Jason smiled, though he knew that his beard almost hid his lips. Her beautiful eyes told him all he needed to know. She knew he was smiling at her, happy to be with her and eager to continue their journey. Their hands touched and fingers twined under the heavy blankets.

Ervin grunted a good morning. "Guess we're up," he growled, "Looks like a nice sunny day, so we should get on our way as soon as possible."

Jason scrambled to his feet He pulled his jeans over the long underwear he wore. "You don't have to come, Ervin. We just need Barry to be our passport. Once we're in the door, he can come home."

The other man laughed shortly. "Hah! You think I'm going to let my boy go out there alone? He already got in enough trouble over there."

"Nope, I'm going." He gave the boy a gentle kick to rouse him. "C'mon, boy, let's go and check out these 'mean' kids."

After a breakfast consisting of hot water, they struck out towards the school. Jason and Monica led, again taking turns breaking their trail through the deep snow. Barry followed reluctantly with his father behind him.

"It's a five-mile walk," Barry panted, "and in this snow, it'll probably take a few hours to get there."

The others nodded grimly and slogged on.

After an hour, they stopped for a short rest. Ervin had fallen behind and now he caught up, red faced and breathing hard.

"Are you okay?" Monica asked with concern.

"Yeah." He answered. "We haven't had much food lately, so I'm not as strong as I used to be."

"Don't worry about me." Ervin continued. "I'll catch up at the school if I fall behind. We have to get there so we can get home before dark."

"It'll be easier coming back," Jason told him. "We'll have this trail to follow. It's tiring breaking through the new snow." He looked at Barry. "You up for this, son?"

The boy nodded. "Yeah. But I still think it's a mistake going over there. I told you these kids are mean and the leader is downright crazy."

Another hour and they could see the square schoolhouse. The three-acre playground surrounding it was smooth and undisturbed. Its many windows blinked and shone in the bright sunshine.

"It looks pretty deserted," Jason said doubtfully. "Are you sure they're here?"

"They hang out mostly in the gym," Barry said. "Follow me." He moved to the front and led them around the building to the windowless gym. The overhang had kept a clear trail close to the walls. He pointed to the double fire doors nervously, then climbed the snow covered steps and paused, waiting for Jason and Monica to join him on the cement landing.

Finally, he squared his shoulders, took a deep breath and pounded on the doors shouting. "Hey, guys! Open the door. It's me!"

After a few minutes, the door opened a few inches and a shaggy head appeared. "Hey, Barry." What're you doing here? Don't you know it's cold out?"

While Barry explained their errand, Monica studied the boy. He appeared to be about sixteen, but under the hair and the grime, it was hard to tell. She could smell wood smoke coming from inside the building.

"Nah!" the boy shook his head. "Ain't no Adnan here. We'd know if there was a brown person around." He laughed.... a laugh that made him seem much older suddenly.

Jason put his hand on the door. "Why don't we come in?" he asked. "We need to warm up before we head back." He gave the door a push and the boy stumbled backwards. Monica and Jason stepped forward pushing Barry out of the way. He looked around him for a moment, then reluctantly followed them in.

As he moved forward, Jason caught a movement from the corner of his eye. He turned his head just in time to see the table leg being swung at his head. He and Monica crashed to the floor while Barry stared in disbelief.

Monica groaned. She tried to bring a hand up to rub her aching head.

"I'm tied up." She shook her head to clear the cobwebs and memory came rushing back. They had stepped into the gym. She had seen a half dozen dirty faces staring back at her, then, nothing. She groaned again as she realized she was tied to a chair with her hands behind her and her feet trussed together.

She still had her coat and boots on, so that was something. Slowly she turned her head and opened her eyes. Jason was tied in the same manner. His head slumped and blood dripped slowly onto his snow pants.

"Good, you're awake." The voice was gruff. A man's voice, not a boy's. She looked up.

There was a makeshift fire pit in the middle of the gym floor. They had found a rim from a tractor tire, and put it directly on the hardwood. Now there was a black circle where it had burned down to the cement. The room reeked of smoke and unwashed bodies. A row of mats lined one wall.

A rough hand grabbed her chin and dragged her head up. She almost cried out at the pain but forced herself to meet her assailant's eyes calmly.

The young man who stared back at her was probably good looking under all that hair and dirt, but now she saw only malice in his expression.

"Who are you?" he asked roughly. His voice was deep and threatening. "What do you want?"

"We're looking for a couple of boys." She answered as she studied the group around the fire. They were all younger than this guy. Some looked as young as twelve or thirteen. She forced her eyes back to his face. "We heard there were some kids hanging around the school, so we thought they might have come here."

He started to speak, but she continued. "One is blond and the other dark. Have you seen them?"

"How did you hook up with Barry?"

She saw Barry huddling with the others. He caught her eye and shook his head slightly.

"He's the same age as Tom and Adnan." She told him. "We know his parents, so we asked them if he had any idea where they would go and he mentioned the school."

"Hah! Mentioned the school did he." He shot an angry look at Barry. "Well did he also tell you that we don't like brown folks and your Adam," he stressed the name, "would not be very welcome here? In fact, he might be in the same spot you're in now."

"And why are we in this spot?" she asked. "We came here and asked a question. All you had to do is say you haven't seen them. Why the dramatics? And by the way, what's your name? I hate talking to someone whose name I don't know."

"Call me Snake." Casually he moved to where Jason still sagged in the chair. "I would've just let you go, but your HERO here," and he lifted

Jason's head by the hair, "wanted to come in." He let go and watched as the unconscious man's neck snapped back down.

"Snake, hey? And I suppose this is your nest of little rattlers? How old are you, Snake?"

"Not that it's any of your business, but I'm eighteen." He smiled a wicked smile. "My nest of rattlers, I like that. You a writer or something?"

"I'm a teacher." She sat up straighter, trying to control her trembling. From the corner of her eye, she saw Jason shift and his hands begin to explore the ropes that were holding them.

He laughed and the other boys joined him. "A teacher! Wow! We hate teachers almost as much as we hate brown people. Don't we, boys?"

A chorus of yeah's, yesses and ok's greeted this statement. Monica glared at the ringleader. She had to keep his attention on her.

"Why do you hate brown people?" she asked. "I'm interested. It's not like we meet a lot of them way up here in the north."

"This is why." He waved his arm to encompass the room. "Everybody knows they'll do anything to take over Canada. They caused the electricity to go out. After we all starve to death they'll just come in and take over."

"You've watched too much conspiracy TV," she told him. "This could have been caused by a giant solar flare."

"But they won't win!" He didn't acknowledge her comment. "We'll still be here. And we're young and tough. When they move in, we'll kill them all." His face came close to hers. "And if they come one at a time, so much the better. Maybe your Adon will turn up."

Monica noticed that Jason's fingers were still busy with the ropes, so she continued.

"His name's Adnan. And he was born in Prince George, so I doubt if he's the guy you're looking for. And how will you be here? You all look pretty hungry to me."

"Don't worry. We know how to survive. Don't we boys?" Another chorus agreed with him. "We go into town and take what we can. And in the spring there will be gardens."

"You're going to plant a garden?" asked Monica. "I'd be interested to know where the seeds will come from since you seem to have taken everything."

"Of course not," he laughed. "We'll just harvest them."

"So, the people who actually plant…what about them?"

"They're mostly old anyway." Snake stood up and moved towards the fire. Jason's hands became still.

"Gimme a drink, will you?" Snake addressed a small boy who immediately leaped to his feet and handed his leader a bottle.

He took a long drink then raised the bottle in a mock salute. "Nobody bothered with the liquor stores," he boasted, "so we were able to take as much as we wanted. The stores are mostly picked over, but sometimes we find a can of something. And…" he leered, "sometimes people have meat lockers or root cellars we can help ourselves to."

When Monica didn't answer he moved closer and looked her over speculatively. "The only thing we don't have here," he said softly. "Is girls. We need girls, don't we boys?"

A few nervous titters answered him. Monica saw Barry drop his head to his chest.

"Why do you kids need girls?" she acted innocent.

Snake threw back his head and laughed loudly. "Yeah, you're right. The KIDS don't need girls." He moved close and began to stroke her face. "But men need girls. And how will we repopulate the world if we don't have girls."

"Why are there no girls here?" Monica was curious. "They must be hungry too. Wouldn't at least a few find their way to this group?" She was aware of an uncomfortable shifting in the room.

"Oh, there were a few." He continued to stroke her face, then started to unbutton her coat. She was helpless to stop him. Next to her, she could feel Jason tense.

"They moved on." He said softly. "Couldn't take the pressure, I guess." His hands were underneath the coat now and he touched her breast.

"You're pretty old." He said. "But a girl is a girl. Right boys?" This time they didn't answer him.

There was a sudden crash as the heavy fire door was flung against the wall. Snake leaped back. The boys scattered as Ervin Dennis roared through the room, swinging an axe in front of him. At the same time, Jason freed his hands and quickly began to loosen the knots tying his feet together.

Monica pushed backwards on the chair to put distance between herself and her tormentor.

He turned towards the raging man, just in time to catch the blade of the swinging axe with his shoulder. He cried out as his arm dropped. The bottle he was holding fell to the floor a moment before he collapsed. Ervin stood over him panting.

"Quick, untie me!" Barry ran across the room and loosened the ropes.

Rubbing her wrists, Monica gave the boy called Snake a nudge with her foot. "I think he'll die." She looked at her husband. "What do you think?"

He nodded.

Ervin kneeled beside the bleeding boy. "Get me something to use as a tourniquet," he told Barry. "We need to stop the bleeding."

His son looked at him in astonishment. "Why?"

"Because I don't want him on my conscience. Now find some rags or give me your shirt or something."

Monica and Jason looked around the now empty gym. The boy at her feet gasped and she looked down at him.

"Tell me your name." she knelt beside Ervin and began to help him remove the blood-soaked shirt.

"Will." He gasped. "William." His eyes were beginning to glaze over. Barry handed his father an old shirt he had found in the corner.

A girl's blouse, Monica noted.

"William what? I need to know for your headstone." Though her voice was sharp, her hands were gentle as she wrapped the arm that Ervin held up for her.

"William Thompson." His breath was coming in short pants. "I don't want to die." Tears ran down his sparsely bearded cheeks.

"Yeah, well, neither does Adnan or those girls you're so proud of." Jason's voice was cold. "Looks like you're on your own. All your little snakes slithered away."

It was an easy matter to rip his tattered shirt off of him. Monica drew in her breath and turned her head away. The swinging axe had gone through his arm and into his thin ribs. Blood pooled beneath him at an alarming rate. And they had nothing to stop it, or to help him.

She stood up and Jason reached out to hold her tight. Ervin continued to kneel by the bleeding body, stroking his forehead and murmuring until William's final gasp. Barry burst into tears.

"I've never seen anyone die." He sobbed into his father's shoulder. "He was an asshole, and I'm not sorry he's gone, but I've never seen anyone die."

Ervin's eyes were sad as he patted his son's back. "It's an awful thing." He commiserated, remembering watching his baby daughter fade away only a few weeks ago.

"Let's move him outside." Jason knelt beside the boy. "We'll come back in the spring and bury him."

"What about those other boys?" Monica asked. "Should we talk to them?"

"We can't save all of them." Jason and Ervin stood by the open door. "They can go home or try to make it here. If they come to our door, we'll take them in, but otherwise, there's nothing we can do."

"Wait!" She looked around for something to wrap Will's body in. "We can't just leave him in a snow bank. What about wild animals?"

Ervin nodded. "This building is probably cold enough to keep him frozen until we can come back. Let's just find a storage closet and leave him there." He raised his voice hoping the other boys were listening. "We're leaving now." He called. "I suggest you all go home before you starve. I don't want anybody to come creeping around my house, or they'll be sorry." He picked up the bloody axe, but Jason held his arm.

"You'd better leave that." He said. "They'll need it to cut wood."

Silently they carried their burden down the school hallway. There was no sign of the other boys as they laid the body in a frigid closet.

"He'll be okay here," Jason told his wife.

The walk back to the Dennis's was made easier by the already cleared trail. After a quick goodbye, they began the trek home. By the time they reached the familiar driveway, the sun had sunk in the west and only the thought of their little son, and how close they had come to never seeing him again, gave them strength.

CHAPTER TWENTY-ONE

Irma was standing anxiously at the front window when she finally saw her son and daughter-in-law trudging down the drive towards their front door. She rushed out and threw her arms around them both.

"We were so worried," she gasped between sobs. "Sam and your Dad were just talking about going to look for you."

Jason hugged her back. "We're glad to be back." He said softly. "What about Tom and Adnan? Are they here?"

"They came back the day after you left." Tony was on the porch now, hugging his son. "They got caught in the storm and had to hole up for a few days."

They stepped into the warm house and the rest of the family gathered around. There were hugs and tears as the travellers were welcomed home. Tom and Adnan hung back sheepishly until they were engulfed in hugs by Jason and Monica.

Ty sat on the couch wrapped in blankets and grinning widely. Monica rushed over to him and gave him a bear hug. "You're better!" she exclaimed.

He nodded and his mother smiled down at him. "He's getting better," Melanie said. "Luckily one of the 'motorcycle gang' is a medical student. He came over with the aspirin and helped us."

"Oh look," Monica looked down at the floor where a puddle of water collected under her boots. "I was so excited, I'm tracking up the house with snow." She began to pull off her boots while Jason came over and rumpled the boy's hair.

"I'm glad you're feeling better, buddy." He swung his own son up out of the playpen. "Jackie, my boy!"

The baby laughed and crowed as he was handed from one parent to the other.

When the excitement had died down and they were all seated at the table, Irma placed bowls of beef soup in front of Jason and Monica.

"The boys next door sent over a side of beef," she told them. "Thank goodness for those cows."

Between slurps, Jason asked Sam, "How are the cattle and horses holding up in this cold weather? It must have been thirty-five below last night."

"Minus thirty-seven," Sam conceded. "The horses are warm enough in the barn, but there is no food for them aside from the hay we managed to get last June when the tractor was still running. The cows are in rough shape. The guys try to go out every day and cull out the ones that look the worst, but I don't know how many will live through the winter."

He wiped his forehead and lowered his eyes, then continued. "It's a good thing those boys came along. The wife and I would never have been able to survive over there."

"We need to send some meat over to the Dennis's." Jason pushed his bowl away. "They have nothing over there and four hungry kids. That's why their oldest got involved with stealing." He went on and told them their story of finding Barry Dennis, the trek to the school and its tragic ending.

When he was finished, everybody was silent for a few minutes.

George looked over at the two teenagers. "You're pretty lucky," he said softly. "That storm might have saved your lives."

"Thanks for looking for us." Adnan dipped his head. "We never should've gone out."

"Damn right." Tony growled. "There's always consequences and these could have been deadly."

"Tomorrow," Tony continued. "you guys can take some meat over to the Dennis's. I'm ashamed we didn't do something before this."

"What could we do?" Irma began to gather up the dishes. 'We didn't know they were in such dire straits, and we have enough to do keeping ourselves alive." She looked around the room. "I mean look at us, we're all thin as rakes and pale as ghosts."

"Of course we'll help them now that we know," she continued. "But we have to keep ourselves alive too." She spoke briskly, but her voice broke on the last words.

Jason stood up and stretched. "I'm going to bed." He announced. "Tomorrow we can discuss how we can help, but right now we're exhausted. Coming, Monica?"

"Yes." She handed Jack over to Stella. "Will you put him to bed? I just don't have the energy."

The baby began to whimper and reached for his Mommy. Stella handed him a soft knitted teddy bear and rocked him soothingly. "Of course, I will. You get some rest and tomorrow things will look better."

"I doubt that," Jason muttered to himself as he climbed the stairs.

"Anybody for a game of cards?" Sam looked around the table. He sighed when nobody agreed. "C'mon" he said bravely. "We can't just sit here and worry. It's too cold to go cut wood and the snow is too deep to hunt, so we're stuck inside for now."

"Okay, we'll play." Adnan shifted his chair. "What about you, Ty. Wanna play?"

"Yeah!" Eagerly the small boy wrapped his blanket around him and climbed onto the nearest chair.

Suddenly Tony looked up from where he had been studying the flames in the fireplace. "It's a new year!" he exclaimed. "I think we missed the fireworks."

The others laughed. "A new year.... what will we have to look forward to, I wonder?"

CHAPTER TWENTY-TWO

George lifted his head from the pillow and considered the gray light coming into the room. Beside him, Melanie sighed and snuggled further into the blankets. Ty sprawled between them, taking up most of the mattress.

Groaning, he pulled himself to his feet. It was getting harder each day to get himself up. Standing, he looked down at his sleeping family. They were so thin they hardly made a bump under the blankets. After adding a log to the fire, he moved to the window and peered out. Soft snow was falling, covering the yard. He saw puddles here and there from the recent thaw. Spring was coming, but it was taking its time.

He decided it was easier to lie on the couch than to go back to bed. He chuckled to himself and thought "go to mattress, more like it." Ty stirred but did not waken. "We're all too weak to get up." His inner grin disappeared as he contemplated the grim truth.

They were surviving on the last of the beef and some rabbits Sam and Tony managed to snare. The ammunition for the twenty-two and the rifle was almost gone. At the farm, most of the cattle had frozen to death in the worst cold the old people could remember. Only the horses had not succumbed. They were thin, but still standing, thank God.

George drifted back to sleep. Outside the snow continued to fall.

It was nearly noon before he woke to the sound of Irma stirring the pot on the heater. She looked up when she felt him watching her.

"Morning," she said. "It's quit snowing, I see."

"That's good." He stood up and stretched. "Maybe we'll see the sun today."

She nodded.

Conversation had waned in the past couple of months. There was nothing more to say and they were all too hungry and worried to keep rehashing the same issues. Between trips to the forest for wood, or to hunt, they slept.

"Grandma Irma," it was Ty, gazing with his big eyes at the pot on the stove. "I'm hungry."

"I know, Honey. Get up and I'll give you a bowl of soup and a drink of water."

The boy sighed and stood up. His thin legs stuck out from a pair of pyjamas that had once belonged to Jason. "I'm so tired." He complained. "And my legs ache."

"I know," Irma and George both averted their faces so he would not see the worry in their eyes. "Maybe your dad can lift you onto the chair if your legs ache. Do you want some soup too, George?"

The big man helped his son onto the chair and shook his head. "No, I'm not hungry right now."

"Liar." Irma filled a bowl for him despite his protest. "You are no good to your family if you starve yourself. You need your strength."

"And," she added, "I think someone should go over and check on the Dennis's again. We haven't seen them for a month."

He shrugged. "What can we do? We have no food to share." He took a sip of the stew, which was more water than meat. "We're all in the same boat."

"I know, I know. But sometimes just the sight of a friendly face can be enough."

The rest of the family shuffled in, one by one and dropped into their accustomed chairs. Everybody looked tired and pale. Only Jack smiled and played, but even he was getting lethargic. Silently they swallowed their soup.

"We'd better go get some more wood," Adnan said finally. "We'll take our guns, and maybe we'll see a deer or something."

Tony nodded. "That's a good idea. The animals will be coming out now. It was a hard winter for them, too so they'll be pretty thin."

"I'll go over and check on the Dennis family," George said, acceding to Irma's request. "Maybe on the way, I'll see some game too." He looked at Jason who was feeding the baby. "Want to come for a walk?"

Jason smiled wryly. "Yeah, like any of us have the strength to go for a walk." He caught his mother's eye, "Okay, okay, I'll go. Beats sitting here waiting to starve, I guess."

Tony slammed his hand on the table. The bowls and spoons jumped and they all looked at him in astonishment.

"We aren't dead yet." He meant to shout, but it came out in a whisper. "As long as we're standing, we'll keep trying. And.." he glared at his son. "We'll help our neighbours as much as we can. If all we can give them is a smile, that's what we'll do."

Stella found her courage and spoke. "It'll be spring soon and we'll be able to find plants to eat. And maybe by the time we plant a garden, this nightmare will be over." She hung her head as Sam gave her a sharp look.

"Don't look at me like that, Sam." She raised her eyes to his. "We've lost everything. The cows are dead, the house is probably destroyed by the motorcycle gang. And we'll probably starve to death like Jason says."

Jason looked alarmed. "I didn't mean it, Stella. I was just feeling a bit down for a minute." He held up his baby son. "Do you think I'll sit around and wait for this guy to fade away like the Dennis baby did?"

"And besides," he leaned forward earnestly. "The motorcycle gang is a bunch of really nice guys and when I saw the house it was as neat as a pin."

"And they've looked after the horses," George added. "I don't know how they kept them alive, but they did."

"Speaking of horses," Sam looked around the table, deliberately avoiding his wife's glare. "Maybe this is a good time to go for a ride. Some news might have filtered into town by now."

"We'll go!" Adnan spoke eagerly. "Me and Tom can ride fast."

Sam laughed. "Have you ever been on a horse?" He smiled at the crestfallen expression on the boy's face. "I thought not. It's harder than it looks, and you have to know the horses. No, I'll go and I think Tony should come with me. We're the oldest and can't really manage the wood carrying anymore. We're the ones who do the least here now."

"Don't say that." Jason and Monica spoke as one. Jason continued. "You two contribute the most with your knowledge of the land and survival. We'd probably have laid down and given up in November if it wasn't for your spirit. And your cows," He added. They all laughed.

"And your mom's garden." Added Tony.

"Which we will see again pretty soon. If we can find some seeds." Irma spoke softly. "But gardens take time, and until then we will have to struggle through. Come on." She stood up. "Let's do something today besides sleep. There's been too much of that lately. And look…" she pointed to the window. "The sun is shining and the snow is melting."

"Can I go outside?" Ty looked up at his mother's worried face. She started to shake her head but was interrupted by Adnan.

"Let him come with us." He ruffled the smaller boy's shaggy hair. "We'll watch him, won't we Tom? And he can carry wood on his sleigh."

"Okay," Melanie didn't have the strength or the will to refuse. "You can go, but dress warm and if you get tired tell Tom and Adnan and they'll bring you in."

"Okay, Mommy." He jumped down; his aching legs forgotten for the moment.

In a few minutes, the boys were on their way to the woods. Ty followed the older boys, pulling his sleigh through the melting snow.

George and Jason soon followed, setting out to the Dennis home. Sam and Tony began a game of cards, having decided to wait until the following day for their adventure.

"I'm going back to bed," Irma told them, and everybody looked at her with worried expressions. "Oh, don't worry." She waved her hand at them. "I know I was the one who said we sleep too much, but it got the young ones out, didn't it?"

The other women agreed and soon followed her up the stairs to their own beds. Melanie laid on the couch and waited for Ty to come back. She was pretty sure he wouldn't last long outside.

CHAPTER TWENTY-THREE

Irma sat up on her bed, awakened by an unfamiliar sound. It sounded like a motor, but they hadn't heard a motor for months. Not since the catastrophe...whatever that was.

Slowly, she pulled her frail body out of bed and towards the window. Outside it had once again begun to snow. The light was fading so it must be late afternoon. The boys should have returned by now, she thought.

Then she heard someone pounding up the stairs. "Mother, Mother, come quick." It was Tony.

She pulled the door open, intending to chide him for running. He was too old for that kind of nonsense. But the look on his face stopped her. His eyes were shining and a smile split his flushed face. He grabbed her hands.

"There's a truck!" he almost shouted at her.

"A truck?" for a moment she was bewildered, then his excitement spilled over onto her. "A truck!" She shook her hands free and ran to the window.

And squealed with delight.

They had never run down the stairs so fast in their lives. Hunger and aches were forgotten as they rushed outside to where the rest of the household stood around an old panel truck. The driver, a man of about fifty dressed for the winter weather in coveralls and a parka was shaking hands all around.

Tony and Irma pushed themselves to the front of the line. They each grasped one of the man's work-worn hands and shook them enthusiastically.

"Where did you come from?"

"Is the power on?"

"Do you have food?"

The questions flew fast and furious until the man stood back and held up his hands, laughing.

"Wait, wait!" He waited until the din subsided. "I don't have food, I'm sorry." Melanie glanced down at Ty despairingly.

"Let's go in," Irma took the man's arm. "come in where it's warm and tell us what's happening. How come you are driving when no vehicles have started for months?"

Everybody trooped up the front stairs, grinning and chattering excitedly. When they were all inside and seated around the heater, the man began.

"I'm Stan," he began. "I live in More's Lake. As you know it's been a brutal winter and last fall my little girl disappeared." Monica and Jason glanced at each other.

"So, I went looking for her, but it's been so cold and I had no food, so I couldn't go far on foot. Eventually, I had to go home and tell my wife I couldn't find her." He shook his head sorrowfully. "We don't know what happened, of course, any more than anyone else. But we survived, I don't really know how, and every once in a while, I would go out to the old truck and try to start it. I figured if something magnetic was stopping the electricity the first thing that would start working was an old motor with no computer stuff on it."

"And sure enough, the old 1985 Ford fired up. We tried the house lights and they still aren't working, but it looks like at least the older cars will run."

Jason stood up and left the room, "I'm going to look for the keys for your truck, Dad."

Irma reached for the phone which had been sitting uselessly on the old fashioned table all winter. "There's a dial tone." She announced excitedly.

The others crowded around, each wanting a turn to listen to what had once been a commonplace sound.

"What about cell phones?" Monica ran upstairs to look for hers.

Melanie began to click the light switch. Nothing happened. "No lights yet." She announced unnecessarily.

"Are you hungry?" Stella looked at Stan with concern. Once he had taken off his outer clothing, they could all see how gaunt he was. "We have beef soup."

His eyes lit up. "You have beef?"

"Yes, but nothing else, I'm afraid," Sam answered while his wife went to get a bowl from the kitchen. "Our cattle have kept us fed all winter, but I think they are all dead now." He shook his head. "It was so cold."

"So, where were you going?" Irma put down the phone.

"I'm still looking for my little girl." Stan began shovelling soup into his mouth, then, looking slightly ashamed, put his spoon down. "Sorry, I forgot my manners. It's been a couple of days since I ate."

"You go ahead and eat." Irma patted his arm. He picked up the spoon again.

As he ate, he studied the room and the people in it. "You have quite a group here." He said.

"Yep." Tony indicated the teenagers who were excitedly whispering in the corner. "Those boys came to us when their families in Prince George couldn't feed them anymore. And George and Melanie found us just before Christmas. That's their little boy. We're all a little skinny, but Sam and Stella kept us and six others alive with their cattle."

Jason came in, stamping the snow from his boots. "I found the keys, Dad. But the battery is frozen. We'll bring it in for a couple of hours, then I think the old truck might start."

"Did you try Mom's car?"

"Yep, but it's new so all those electrical and computer systems still don't work."

Monica had returned, carrying her cell phone. "No luck here, either." She announced.

"Makes sense." George nodded. "Landlines are just what they say...landlines. They work on wires. Cell phones, computers, they all depend on satellites. So maybe whatever knocked everything out affected the satellites. And remember," he held up one finger. "Even if systems work, they need maintenance and people. I imagine that will take a long time to start up."

"Do you think the government and the military will still be workable?" Stan asked.

"Who knows. With no transportation, lots of people would have been stuck wherever they landed. All we can hope is that someone somewhere is trying to fix things."

Stan had finished his soup and now reached for his coat. "Well," he said. "I'm grateful for the food. But I still have to find my daughter."

"Wait." Jason stopped him. "I think we might know what happened to her. Maybe you should sit down."

He looked at Melanie. "If you don't want Ty to hear this, you might want to take him upstairs, Mel."

She nodded and taking Ty by the hand led him into the kitchen. "Come on, buddy. We'll go and clean up the dishes."

"What dishes?" he complained. "We haven't eaten yet."

"Well then, we'll have some soup." She tugged his hand and he reluctantly followed her out of the room, looking longingly back.

"What is it?" Stan had sat back down. "Do you know where she is?"

"Maybe," and Jason told him of the boys at the school and Snake's boast about stealing girls.

Monica reached over and grasped Stan's hand. "We don't know if what they were saying was true," she said softly. "but we did find a girl's blouse on the floor."

Stan's face was white. "Where is this school?" he asked through gritted teeth. "I'll kill them if they hurt my daughter."

"I'm afraid you're too late for that," Jason told him the rest of the story, about their rescue by Ervin and the tragic consequence.

Stan's shoulders slumped.

Then he straightened up. "But you don't know if it was Tara, do you?" he asked.

"No, we don't." Monica again reached for the clenched fist between them. "Why don't you stay here tonight? The road is still covered with snow. Tomorrow morning, Jason and George will go with you."

Jason nodded. "That's a good idea. We'll get a good night's sleep and start out fresh. You can't get very far tonight."

"I made it this far," Stan answered. But then he acceded. "I'll appreciate the help."

Darkness now enveloped the house. After a small bowl of soup each, Stan told them of his trip from More's Lake. He had stopped at every house he saw, sometimes having to walk in through deep snow. In one house he had found three bodies, a woman and two small children, lying together in a bed.

Two of the houses had been empty. He assumed everybody had been away from home when the power quit.

In three houses, he had found people alive but defensive. One man had threatened him with a gun.

"I didn't see your farm." He answered Sam when asked. "It must be off the main road."

"Yeah, it is." Sam nodded. "That's why we could keep our animals as long as we did."

"Ten miles in three days." Jason shook his head. "Would have been faster to walk."

"Probably." Stan agreed. "But that old truck kept me warm and it proved that things are going to get better. And besides," he added. "I made a lot of side trips checking houses."

"That's true!" Irma and Tony stood up. "Tomorrow is the start of getting back to normal. You'll find Tara, drive over to the farm and start spreading the word."

"But now…bed. Stan, you can bunk in the attic with the boys. They sleep right up by the chimney so that's the warmest place in the house. We'll spread some blankets on the floor for a bed." Irma pointed at Adnan. "C'mon boys. Big day tomorrow. Show Stan where you sleep."

Obediently they all headed off to bed, even though sleep would be elusive.

CHAPTER TWENTY-FOUR

Dawn was breaking when the family once again met in the living room. George, yawning widely, filled the old heater with logs, making the room almost too hot.

A low murmur of excitement ran through the gathering.

It was coming to an end. More than the watery sun, hope shone on the horizon.

Jason carried the battery out to where the old truck was parked. "I hope this works," he muttered to Stan.

"Don't you have jumper cables?"

"Somewhere. Dad has everything around here somewhere. They weren't really a priority up until now."

They finished hooking up the battery cables and Jason turned the key. The motor turned over once, then died.

"Try it again." Stan fumbled under the hood.

The key turned smoothly, the motor rumbled, hesitated, then roared to life.

"That old truck never let me down." Tony walked towards them and they all grinned. Jason jumped out of the driver's seat.

"How much gas do you think there is?"

"I dunno." Tony looked around the yard. "We can always siphon from the car. And if there's enough to get to the farm, there will be gas in the tractor."

Everybody was outside now, coats unbuttoned and boots slipped carelessly on. It was definitely getting warmer. Monica carried the baby who blinked in the sunlight.

Stan shook hands with the men and hugged the women. He tousled Ty's hair. "Thanks for everything." He said. "The food and the information."

"I'm coming with you." Monica handed Jack to his grandmother. "If you find Tara, you might need a woman along."

"Good point." Jason gave her a one armed hug. "Are you dressed warm enough?"

"Are you going to stop at the Dennis's?" Irma asked anxiously.

"We'll go to the school first and see how things are there." Jason and Monica climbed into the van's front seat. Stan had it running and was ready to get going. At the last minute, George jumped into the cargo area. He was carrying the twenty-two and a shovel.

"Just in case," he smiled. "You never know when we need to clear a road."

As they drove away, Tony looked at his friend, Sam. "Let's go, Sam. I think I can still remember how to drive this thing."

"Should we come?" Tom asked. "You might need help shovelling too."

"Sure, why not? Run and get those two snow shovels on the porch, and make sure you have gloves." He winked at Sam. "Might as well let the young guys do the hard stuff."

"Can I come?" Ty pulled on his sleeve. "I can shovel too."

Tony gave him a kind glance then bent down to be at eye level. "There isn't room in the truck for you, little man. And someone has to be here to be the man of the house." Melanie snorted. "You stay here and keep watch, okay."

Ty nodded solemnly. "Okay, Grampa. I'll be the man."

"Good," Tony stood up and patted his head. He climbed into the driver's seat, Sam beside him. The two teenagers climbed into the box. They pulled their parkas up around their ears and wrapped their mittened hands around their guns.

After waving them away, the women returned to the warmth of the house. Somehow, even though there was still no food, lights or propane, everything looked brighter.

"You know what?" Irma asked. "I can phone Flora Dennis."

"Should you?" Stella smiled. "You might give them all heart attacks."

"Let's try. If we have a dial tone, they should too." Quickly Irma punched in the familiar number. She could hear it ringing, one. Two…five times. Then a tentative voice at the other end.

"He..e..lo."

"Flora. This is Irma." There was a loud clunk as the receiver fell. Then she could hear crying. "The phone works. Ervin, the phone works! Quick, try the light switch."

Irma waited patiently until the voice returned. "Irma, is it really you? Is the power on over there?"

"It's me, Flora. The landlines work and the older vehicles, the ones without computers, will start. But still no lights."

The voice changed to Ervin's. "The car started? Is this nightmare ending?"

"I don't know," Irma admitted. "But you should see Jason and Monica sometime today. They'll tell you the whole story. I just couldn't wait."

"Okay, kids, settle down." He was talking to his family now. "Thanks so much, Irma. Poor Flora is overwhelmed, she's sitting here crying. I'm going out to see if my car will start." He hung up abruptly and Irma slowly replaced the receiver.

"Well?" Stella and Melanie were watching her.

She smiled happily. "They thanked me for calling and Ervin is going out to see if his car will start." She shook her head. "Isn't that just like a man? The first thing is to get those wheels turning."

CHAPTER TWENTY-FIVE

It was noon before the school came in sight. They had all spent their fair share of time jumping in and out of the truck and shovelling. In the warmer weather, the snow had melted in some areas, but drifts had built up as much as four feet in the shaded places.

Now, as they surveyed the unbroken snow around the school, they were exhausted from the strenuous exercise.

"It doesn't look like anyone is here," Stan spoke first. "When were you here?"

"Christmas," Monica spoke softly.

"Let's go in." George clambered out of the back of the truck and began to make his way towards the glassed front doors.

The others followed in his wake.

They cleared the steps and pulled on the door, which opened easily.

"Not locked?" All four of them looked around uneasily. "They should be locked."

"The kids were hanging around here for months," Monica said. "They probably wouldn't worry about locking doors."

"Well, I hope someone is still hanging around," Stan growled. "I want to ask them some questions."

"They were in the gym."

Cautiously they made their way through the dark hallways. It was colder in here than outside. Classroom doors stood open allowing light to stream in and giving the floor a striped appearance. They glanced into each empty room as they passed.

"It's awfully quiet." Jason stopped short, causing a small collision. "I don't think anyone's here."

"Maybe they all went back to their homes after their ringleader was gone," Monica answered.

"Why are you whispering?" George whispered.

"I don't know. We don't want to scare anybody away?"

"There's nobody here." Stan's voice echoed through the empty halls. "Let's finish checking all the rooms and get out of here."

"Open all the doors." Jason tried the door to what looked like a storage closet. "We need to find out if Tara was here."

Methodically they began to open doors, glancing into storage areas, closets and bathrooms. William's body was where they had left it.

They gave him a cursory glance then moved on to the gym. There was a circle in the middle of the floor where Monica and Jason had seen the fire.

"They're lucky they didn't burn the whole building down around them." George walked towards the makeshift fire pit. "That explains why there are no desks in the classrooms. They burned them all."

He circled the area and kicked absently at a pile of what looked like old curtains. Then he leaned closer.

"Whoa!" he drew back. "I think I found one of the boys."

He lifted a corner of the curtain, exposing the face of a child. He grimaced and looked more closely around the large room.

"What is it?" Monica approached him but stopped when he held up his hand.

"Don't look." He told her. "This kid can't be more than thirteen. And look." He waved his arm, indicating eight more bundles on the floor. "It looks like they all just laid down as close to the fire as they could get and died."

Monica's eyes filled. "We should have helped them." She ran across the floor and flung open the outer doors. Light streamed in. "We could have helped them!" she screamed. "They are just babies and we walked away and left them."

She sank to the floor, sobbing uncontrollably.

Jason sat beside her and reached to grab her hand. She pulled it away and glared at him through her streaming eyes. "You said to leave them." She accused. "You said we couldn't help, but they're just kids. We shouldn't have left them."

"Think, Monica." He wiped his own tears away. "They ran away from us. They had stolen our food. When we were here they still had some of it. What could we have done? If we took them home with us we might all be dead too. We're barely hanging on as it is. Would you take food from Jack or Ty, to feed them?"

"I don't know." She was calming down and let him put his arm around her. "It's just wrong to leave children."

"I know, I know. It's awful, but really, I can't see how we could have done anything else."

They both looked up as Stan stood over them, blocking the light from the open doors. "No Tara." He ran a hand down his face. "I looked, they're all boys."

"I don't know if I should be happy or sad about that." He continued. "She doesn't appear to have been here, but then, where is she?"

George was still standing by the first body he had found. "What should we do with them?" he asked. "It doesn't seem right to just leave them here."

"As long as it's cold," Jason stood up, "They'll be okay here. But we'll have to come back and bury them before it gets much warmer."

"We should bring in Snake too." Monica got to her feet, still crying, but softly now. "We don't know who they are and maybe someone will come looking just like Stan did."

"I know him," Stan said thoughtfully as they carried the body in. "I think he used to live down the street from us."

"His name was William Thompson," Monica said as they lowered him to the floor.

As he leaned over, the blanket that had been wrapped around William came loose and his upper body was exposed.

Stan reached over and grabbed the white blouse that had been used to staunch the blood. "What's this?" He held it up to the light.

"It was all we could find at the time." Monica stepped forward and tried to take it from his hand. "It was laying on the floor so I grabbed it."

Stan's face had gone a ghastly shade of green. "It's Tara's." he croaked. "It was her favourite shirt. She was here."

He looked around wildly, ignoring the body that lay at his feet. "She's here. We have to find her."

Monica touched his arm but he didn't feel it through his thick coat. "If she was here,' she said gently, "It's too late. All the boys are gone."

Suddenly he began to kick the body of William Thompson. "I knew it! This guy lived down the street. He was always causing trouble with his fancy car and his rowdy friends. Where is my daughter?" He reached down and began to shake the body. "Where is she, you son of a bitch?"

"Stan. Stan." The two men each took one of his arms and tried to restrain him. "It's too late. He can't tell you."

Finally, he let the body fall with a crash. Monica quickly replaced the blanket.

"Let's get out of here." George and Jason led the other man towards the exit sign. "We'll come back in a couple of days and look more closely. And we'll bury these poor boys."

"Poor boys!" Stan spat. "They killed my girl. They deserve whatever hell they are in now." His shoulders began to shake and he clung to the blood-stained shirt. "How am I going to tell my wife?"

They left him sobbing on the cement steps and quickly moved all the bodies into one corner of the gym.

When they were done, they closed the doors and made their way back to the truck. There, George took the keys and they slowly made their way homeward.

"Should we stop at the Dennis's?" Monica whispered to her husband.

He shook his head.

"I don't think Stan is up to meeting anyone else right now." He replied softly. "We can come over tomorrow in Dad's truck. It'll be easier now that we cleared the road."

They were riding in the cargo bay, leaving the passenger seat for Stan. Now, they huddled together, trying to forget the gruesome sight left behind in the school gym. Monica sobbed and Jason held her tenderly.

CHAPTER TWENTY-SIX

"Did you find her?" Tony looked inquiringly at his son.

The answer came in the slumped posture and glum expressions on their faces.

"Oh." Tony closed the door as the group stepped off the porch into the house. "I'm sorry, Stan." He patted the man's shoulder awkwardly.

Only Stella with her knitting and the baby were in the living room. Monica scooped him up and he laughed delightedly. "Where is everybody?" Monica asked.

"They are all laying down." Stella set aside her needles and wool. "Nobody has any strength, and it's getting colder again, so sleeping seemed a good option." She smiled at the mother and baby. "I volunteered to watch Jack. He's the only one who didn't like the idea of a nap."

The men stamped into the living room, holding their cold hands out to the heater. "It is getting colder again." George agreed. "Spring in the north, I guess."

"Is there anything to eat?" Jason looked into the pot that always sat on top of the heater. "Did the guys at the farm have anything?"

"Yep, we brought back some more meat, and Adnan managed to bag a couple of grouse. They're hanging in the shed right now. We'll cook them tomorrow." Tony set some bowls on the table.

Stan was still standing in the doorway. Now he reached for his coat. "I think I'll go." He said. "I have to get home and tell my wife that I didn't find Tara."

"Don't go yet." Tony stepped between him and the door. "Have something to eat. It's getting dark too. Wait until morning and we'll pack up some meat for you to take home with you."

"No, no. I can't take any more of your supplies." He looked around the room, crowded with the long table, heater, rolled-up mattresses and the old couch. "You have enough people to feed."

"At least eat first." Jason pushed a steaming bowl into his hand. "You won't be any help to your wife if you're passing out with hunger. And Dad's right. Wait until morning. What if something happens on the road? How much gas do you have?"

Stan held up his hands helplessly and tried to smile. "Okay, okay. Point taken. I'll wait until morning. But I can't take any of your food."

"Pish posh," Stella came and took hold of his hand. "I don't know what you found over there, but you look terrible. At least here you'll be warm and you can tell us what's been happening in town all winter."

The six of them were sitting around the table, and listening to Stan tell them of the shortages in town, and the desertion of the RCMP when Irma crept down the stairs and joined them. Seeing her come into the room, Monica was shocked at how small and frail she looked. After a day away, her deterioration was obvious to the younger woman.

"What's the matter, hon?" Jason asked, seeing her eyes suddenly fill.

"Nothing." She wiped them away. "It's just been a stressful day. Here you take Jack, and put him to bed later, will you." She stood up. "I'm going to bed too. Goodnight all." She bent and kissed her mother-in-law on the top of her gray head. "G'night, Mom."

Irma watched her disappear up the stairs then gave Jason a questioning look. "What's that about?" she asked. He shrugged in answer, and she joined them at the table.

"Soup?" Tony asked as he made a move to stand and get it for her.

"No, I'm sick of the taste of it."

"You have to eat."

"I will. Just not right now. Sit down, Dear. I didn't mean to interrupt Stan." She turned towards their guest. "Did I hear you say that the RCMP deserted the town? Just like that?"

"Not just like that." He temporized. "They were all there until about October. Then it started to get cold and I guess they were worried about their own families, so they started drifting away. The chief stayed, but he was so overwhelmed, he ended up committing suicide."

"How awful!" Irma covered her mouth with her hand.

"When was that young cop here, Mother?" asked Tony. "The guy on a horse."

She wrinkled her forehead in concentration. "I think it was about September. Remember, we were in the garden getting the rest of the potatoes out."

For a moment, she stopped, remembering the taste of those potatoes. Then she sighed heavily and continued. "He was a nice young guy, but you could see he was just overwhelmed. And he didn't have any information."

"Yeah. They borrowed a couple of horses and tried to contact people around the countryside. But they didn't bring the horses back. Just decided to keep going, I guess. Figured they'd be able to cope better somewhere else." George said.

He took a deep breath. "By Christmas the police station was empty. I know there are at least four cops still in town, but they're just as hard up as the rest of us. Not really much crime after the initial emptying of the stores and a few houses broken into."

Jason's voice was grim. "Yeah, well we know there was some crime. Those boys at the school were busy stealing every bit of food they could find. I have a feeling we'll find all sorts of other stuff at the school too."

"I'll come back in a couple of weeks when the snow is gone." Stan stood up. "But now, I need to get a good night's sleep so I can get an early start."

He bent over Irma and gave her a quick kiss on the cheek, then did the same to Stella. "Thanks, ladies. I appreciate the bed and food. If I don't see you in the morning, I'll be back in a few weeks."

When they heard his heavy footsteps climbing the stairs, Irma turned to Tony and said, "Pack up that beef you brought back and put it in his truck right now. I don't want him leaving without it. We can eat the grouse tomorrow and the boys can get us some wild game in the next few days."

"I think we should go to town too." Tony left to do his wife's bidding. Jason continued. "I want to go to some of the stores and see if there are any seed packets around. When people were looking for food, they may have left the seeds. Without them, we won't have anything to plant and I have a feeling we're on our own for a while yet."

The others nodded. In their remote corner of the world they were going to be the last to hear of any improvement in the country's situation.

"I feel like it's 1850 again." Stella stood up and stretched. "Back to the dark ages."

By seven in the evening, the household was asleep. Nobody heard the coyotes howling or saw the snow coating the ground again.

CHAPTER TWENTY-SEVEN

"Look what I found." Monica came into the kitchen and handed Irma a battered book. She glanced over without interest and continued washing a cup under the running water.

"Another book? I thought you had read every book in the house three times by now."

"Yes, I thought so too. But I was digging in the attic and found this one. Look at the title."

"Edible Plants in the North". Irma read. "Published in 1929. Wow!" She dried her hands on the tattered dishtowel that hung on the useless oven and reached for the book. "Let's see that."

She opened the front cover and saw the faded name written in an old fashioned script. "This belonged to Dad's grandmother." She looked up at her tall daughter-in-law. "Now this is a useful find."

Monica laughed. It had been three weeks since Stan had visited them in his old truck. The forest and fields were greening around them. "Now we'll know what plants to look for. Isn't it great?"

Irma sat down. Since the weather had warmed up, they had moved the table back into the kitchen. The old heater which had served them so well was still kept burning, but that was for cooking, not heat. While nights were cool, the days were lengthening and warming. Birds tweeted and trilled in the woods. Sam and Stella were talking about moving back to the farm.

Monica took the book back and leafed through it. "I'm going to make a list and then put on my boots and go hunting. I'll take Jack for a walk too."

Irma looked over her shoulder and pointed to one of the pictures. "Look, we can eat thistles. Who knew? And dandelions. We have lots of them. What else?"

The back door opened and Melanie came in with Ty trailing behind her.

"The men are back." She told them.

"Oh good. I hope they found some seeds in town." Irma stood up with difficulty. The winter had been hard on her old bones. The two younger women looked at her with concern.

She waved them away when they pressed her to stay in the kitchen. "No, no, I'm excited to hear the news. Let's go outside."

On the porch, Jason met her and handed her a bundle of seed packets. "When you're ready." He grinned.

"Not when I'm ready," she replied tartly. "When the ground is ready. And that won't be for almost another month. Did you find anything else?"

Tony's face was grim. "We found lots of trouble," he said. "Let's sit out here and we'll fill you in." They all took seats on the porch. Tom and Adnan came from the direction of the barn and joined them, perching on the steps.

"How did the truck run?" Monica asked.

"Good. We stopped at the farm and got some gas out of the tractor. It was kind of a bouncy ride, and we thought poor George was going to bounce right out of the box, but he managed to hang on."

They all laughed and George made a show of rubbing his skinny backside.

"There were cars all over the road." Jason sobered. "When everything stopped so suddenly, lots of people just crashed into each other." He glanced at Ty who was quietly rolling his matchbox cars back and forth on the step. "I asked Stan how he managed to get through and he said he just went around as much as possible."

"Lots of people didn't make it out." He lowered his voice. "Some had crawled onto the road, and the animals had got to them."

"But most of the cars were empty," George added hastily. "So those people obviously got out and went somewhere on foot."

Jason nodded. "I'm glad we all decided to go. We had to push our way through in a few places."

"Quite an adventure." Tony nodded solemnly.

"Did you see Stan?" Irma asked.

"Yep, we dropped in on him and his wife." Jason paused. "She's a nice lady, but in complete despair about their daughter. Apparently, Tara had quite a crush on this Snake guy, so she thinks it wouldn't have been hard for him to convince her to go with him."

"Poor woman." Irma sighed. "But I'm glad Stan made it home okay through the snowstorm."

"I guess he had quite a trip." Jason said. "After he left here it turned into a full blown blizzard. If he hadn't had his own tracks to follow back, he might still be sitting in a snowbank somewhere."

"I'm glad you decided to wait." Melanie patted her husband's hand. "It would have been even worse for you in the back of that truck." They all laughed as George rubbed is bony hip again.

"There is virtually nobody healthy in town. They all looked at us like we were crazy when we asked them if they had any news about the power. Then we went to the police station to see if anyone was there. There wasn't but just as I walked in the phone rang and I talked to some guy in Vancouver." Jason paused.

"And?" Everybody was on the edge of their seats.

"And…he said Vancouver is up and running. The power companies are fixing lines as fast as they can. The police and military are getting ready to move in and set up relief stations." They all began to talk at once, but Jason held up his hand. "But remember where we are. It's over six hundred miles. It'll be a long time before they get to us. We still need to look after ourselves."

"We need to go home." Tom looked at Adnan. "We need to go home and see how our families are." Adnan nodded in agreement.

"Now we have wheels, "Jason told them, "I'll drive you. We can be there in a couple of hours, depending on the roads. I'm hoping that as we get closer to Prince George they will have been cleared."

"But what happened?" Irma cried. "They just can't pretend that everything is back to normal with no explanation. What happened?"

"It was an accident."

"An accident?" Stella's voice was shrill. "An accident that killed thousands, maybe millions of people.?"

"An accident."

"Have you heard of HAARP?" asked Jason.

"That old conspiracy theory?" said Monica. "We talked about that a couple of months back."

Jason shook his head. "Apparently it's real. The conspiracy theory was that the government was trying to control the weather or something. But it actually is a satellite array, which the American government uses to analyze the ionosphere. At least that's what they said. What the guy on the phone told me is that when they were shooting lasers into the sky, somehow it caused a huge flare, almost like a solar flare, and POOF! No power. And it wasn't just North America. It was worldwide."

Monica shook her head and held tight to her son.

"An accident!"

"Yep. A massive accident." Jason grinned wryly. "Oh, and for what it's worth, the USA has apologized to the world for this terrible incident."

Everybody was silent as they digested this.

After a moment, Tony snorted and stood up. "An incident!"

"Well come on everybody. We can't sit here worrying. We still need wood for the stove and meat for the pot. Let's get busy."

EPILOGUE

Tony and Irma rocked gently and watched as their small grandson chased a butterfly around the yard. If she turned her head, Irma could see her son and his wife bent over in the garden. Tom and Adnan could be heard behind the house, arguing over who was going to look after the puppy.

She smiled at her husband and he said, "I feel you looking at me." He opened one eye. "What are you thinking?"

"Oh, you know what I'm thinking." She gave his knee a gentle slap. "You always do."

He laughed and closed his eye again. "You're thinking that we were very lucky. Here we are with our family all around us."

He sat up straight and continued softly. "It's too bad Tom and Adnan couldn't find their parents though."

Now it was Irma's turn to close her eyes.

"Yes, I know. We did all we could and Jason and George even went door to door in their neighbourhood looking for them, but they have disappeared. Like so many others." She sighed.

"Well, he did find the puppy and her dam in one of the abandoned houses. Against all odds, she managed to get through the winter." He grinned. "The boys do love that dog." He glanced down at the collie at his feet.

"She needs a better name than 'mommy' though." Irma laughed just as the phone gave a shrill ring. "That'll be Stella." She said. "They are happy to be back in their own house, but I think she's lonesome over there since the motorcycle gang left." She gave him a nudge with her foot. "While I'm talking to her, why don't you light the fire?"

"Okay." He struggled to his feet. The winter had been hard and he was feeling every year of his seventy. "I'll be glad when the power is back on and we don't have to depend on wood anymore."

"There still won't be any propane." His wife pointed out. "It might be years before it's being delivered up here in the bush."

"You can get George to help you get more wood when he and Melanie get back from town." She called over her shoulder. "Hi, Stella." Her voice grew softer and Tony made his way to the edge of the verandah.

Jason waved at him from the garden and he waved back. He could see Jack running across the yard, calling for Tom and Adnan, his big brothers.

He sighed again, then smiled. It would be another hard year coming up, but they were all together. He leaned down and picked one of the roses that were growing up the railing, patted his new canine companion on the head and turned towards the front door.

"Come on, mommy dog. Let's go see what's for supper."

FINIS

About J.M Johnson

J.M. Johnson lives outside of Edmonton, Alberta, Canada. She grew up in northern B.C. where the incident is set. She enjoys watching the birds outside her window, especially in the spring when the earth is waking up.

Check out her website **www.jmjohnson-author.com**

Personal note:

Thank you for purchasing my book. I hope you have enjoyed reading about the Baldini family. If so, please post a review on Amazon or Goodreads. I read all comments, and appreciate the feedback. Scroll down for an introduction to more of the incident's effects. ***"What Happened to Tara."***

WHAT HAPPENED TO TARA
PROLOGUE

Stan Morrisson hammered on his daughter's bedroom door. "C'mon, Tara. Today is the day. Rise and shine."

Only silence greeted him, so Stan shrugged and continued down the stairs. He shivered in the early morning chill. As he entered the dark kitchen, Miriam gave him an enquiring look.

"Are they up?"

"Danny is, but Tara's pulling her usual teenage shit. I'll go up and roust her again in a few minutes."

His wife stuffed another jar of fruit into her basket. "I wish we didn't have to go," she said. "If only the lights would come back on and we could go back to normal."

Stan hugged her tightly and she leaned against his chest. "I wish we didn't have to go, too," he said. "But you know we'll be better off on the farm. Ever since that EMP, or bomb, or whatever it was killed all the power last month, things are getting worse every day."

She patted his arm and gave a weak smile. "I know. But maybe Tara's right and we should wait a few more days. It's a long walk to the farm."

"It is a long walk," Stan agreed. "That's why we can't waste any time. Besides I want to make sure my parents are okay."

They stepped apart and Miriam commented, "I could have sworn I left a bag of apples on the counter last night. I thought we could eat them on the way. We'll have to pick some more before we go."

"Maybe they're in the pantry." Stan turned towards the stairs ready to warn his twelve-year-old son about running in the house when Danny shouted.

"She's gone! Tara's gone!"

"What do you mean, she's gone?" Miriam turned and stared at him. "Where would she go?"

Stan ran up the stairs, taking them three at a time. He burst through the bedroom door, the door with the princess crown still on it from when she was three, and stopped in confusion. The bed hadn't been slept in. Its covers were pulled tight and the pillows were undisturbed. The closet door stood open, a jumble of shoes and bright coloured clothes spilling out. The top of her dresser was uncluttered, cleared of the usual lipsticks and make-up.

"It looks like she was packing." He started to say, but Miriam cut him off. "Her backpack is gone. It was right on that chair by the window."

Stan ran his palm over his bearded chin. "That crazy girl. She's probably hiding somewhere, hoping we'll change our minds about going to my parent's farm." He reached for his wife's hand, but she had moved to the closet and was surveying its contents.

"Typical teenager. Nearly the end of September and she's wearing sandals." She rummaged through the mess on the floor, then pulled one of the dresser drawers open "I don't know what she was thinking." She continued. "None of her sweaters have been packed, but she took her bathing suit." Her voice faded and Stan stepped closer.

He reached for her hand but was interrupted by Danny thundering back up the stairs. "Her coat is gone," he reported. "And her winter boots."

All three of them gazed out the window at the late fall flowers blooming through stalks of uncut grass. A few leaves on the birch tree across the street showed a touch of gold. Winter was not far away in Northern B.C. Even in mid-September, it was already knocking at the door.

Miriam swallowed the lump that was forming in her throat. "Why would she take her coat and boots and leave her sweaters?" She slammed the drawer closed. "Doesn't she know how worried we'll be?"

"She can't have gone far." Stan rubbed his chin thoughtfully. "I'll go look around the neighbourhood. Danny, you get on your bike and check with all her friends. Somebody will have seen her."

Danny nodded. "I'll try, Dad, but most of her friends have already left town. Everybody's running South."

"Yeah, I know." His dad patted his shoulder. "That's what we're trying to do too. Do your best, son."

"I should have paid more attention." Miriam said softly "Obviously she was more upset than we thought."

Stan grunted. "Oh, I think we knew how she felt. I think the whole neighbourhood knew after that screaming match you two had."

"She's scared." Tears came to Miriam's eyes. "That's all. If I hadn't been so busy, I might have reassured her more."

The door slammed behind Danny as Stan was shrugging his shoulders into his coat. "Don't blame yourself, Hon. We're all scared. Besides," he gave her a quick hug. "We've all been working like dogs, she knew that. I'll find her and drag her ass home. When your sister gets here, tell her we're leaving tomorrow instead."

Where has Tara gone and what happened after she disappeared?

Manufactured by Amazon.ca
Bolton, ON